CURFEW

Curfew

& Other

Eerie Tales

by

Lucy M. Boston

Swan River Press
Dublin, Ireland
MMXXI

Curfew & Other Eerie Tales
by Lucy M. Boston

Published by
Swan River Press
Dublin, Ireland
in September, MMXXI

www.swanriverpress.ie
brian@swanriverpress.ie

Cover design by Meggan Kehrli
from "The Woman at the Window"
by Elisabeth Vellacott (c. 1944)

Set in Garamond by Ken Mackenzie

Hemingford Grey Manor logo
by Peter Boston

Paperback Edition
ISBN 978-1-78380-746-8

Swan River Press published
a hardback edition of
Curfew & Other Eerie Tales in August 2011.

Contents

Introduction

Lucy M. Boston is best remembered today for her children's novels set in Green Knowe, the ancient, haunted house based on Hemingford Grey Manor near Huntingdon, Cambridgeshire, where she spent most of her adult life. She began writing these charming, sometimes chilling, tales when she was already in her sixties. But they were not her first attempts at fiction. A handful of supernatural tales dating from the early 1930s[1] exist among her papers. Of the short stories in this volume only three have been published before— "Curfew", "The Tiger-Skin Rug" and "Many Coloured Glass"—all having appeared originally in long out of print anthologies for children.

This hardly seems to do them justice. Children play pivotal roles in the first two—and best—of those stories, it's true, but there is nothing specifically juvenile about their language or themes, nothing to exclude them from a mature bookshelf. Indeed in her use of children as witnesses and victims of the supernatural, Boston was— consciously or otherwise—emulating that other great East Anglian supernaturalist, M. R. James (1862-1936).[2]

---

[1]   Phillippa Pearce, who knew Boston, well records that "The Tiger-Skin Rug" was one of several ghost stories that Boston wrote in 1933.

[2]   One thinks of "Lost Hearts" or "A School Story", the latter of which has appeared in two of the volumes in which Boston's supernatural tales have been anthologised.

Boston's debt to James in fact runs deep. The stories collected here offer the same unmistakeable, inexplicable malice that we find in James, and the same lurking feeling of terror: what Boston calls in "Curfew" the "thrill, or chill, of expectation". And like James's most celebrated stories, most of those collected here centre around antiquarian objects—an old bell, a rug bought at auction, an intricately carved desk left in a house by a previous occupant—curious *trouvés*, artefacts of the past that carry more than memories with them. This interaction of the tangible past with the present, which is central to the antiquarian ghost story, was to become a major theme in Boston's later children's books.

Both authors share a gift for the memorable and haunting phrase. In "Curfew", for example, when the narrator recalls a ghastly face that looks in at him as he plays hide-and-seek in the garden, the description recalls James at his most eerily vivid: "His hair and cheeks were clotted with earth, through which his yellow teeth showed more on one side than the other, his eye sockets were appallingly hollow, and he lifted his chin as the blind do when they seek."[3]

Devotees of M. R. James will be familiar, too, with the soundscape that Boston creates: the "Curfew" bell is unforgettably terrible, of course, but more directly Jamesian perhaps is this description from "The Tiger-Skin Rug": "That night was the first night on which we heard the howling. Everybody knows how a cat can make one's spine creep, but this was far worse and all the more eerie for be-

---

[3] This knack for describing faces never left Boston. In her first volume of autobiography, *Memory in a House* (1973), she brilliantly describes a much-loved old housekeeper as having "the sort of face that might peer round a mushroom".

ing low and searching. It woke both of us up; my wife sat bolt upright in bed."[4]

That Boston was familiar with James's work—and shared something of his sense of humour—is confirmed in her second volume of memoirs, *Perverse and Foolish* (1979), where she recalls an ill-favoured male relative: "a widower-in-law, a tall tottering zombie who qualified for Monty James's scholar whose eye sockets were covered in cobwebs." The reference is to "The Tractate Middoth", which opens with a memorable apparition in Cambridge University Library.

Boston and James in fact both lived within a short distance of each other in Cambridge, for a brief time, during the early part of the First World War, and her memoirs offer the tantalising possibility that they might have met. In 1915 she lodged for a while, with her brother Jas, in a flat on King's Parade in Cambridge and recalls a daily ritual: "I went every evening to Evensong in King's Chapel, then as yet unembellished and overwhelmingly beautiful. The sound of King's Bell at 5.15 calling us in, is still the most evocative sound I know."

In 1915 M. R. James was the Provost of King's and showed a great interest in the running of the Chapel. It's inconceivable that he didn't occasionally attend Evensong. Might the twenty-three year old Lucy have sometime gathered up the courage to speak to the affable, bespectacled Provost? He was a well-known literary figure by then. She must surely at least have recognised him.

But Boston was never simply the slavish imitator of a more celebrated author. Her imagination and voice are

---

[4]   Read James's "The Ash Tree" and "An Episode of Cathedral History" if this kind of thing works for you.

distinct and original, and the settings of these tales, if not the events they narrate, are born of her own experiences.

Lucy Maria Wood was born in Southport, Lancashire, on 10 December 1892. After attending a boarding school in Sussex and a finishing school in Paris, she went up to Somerville College, Oxford, in 1914 to read English. She left, before taking her degree, to train as a nurse and worked in a French military hospital in Paris during the second half of the First World War. In 1917 she returned to England and married Harold Boston, whose father had married a cousin of Lucy's after his mother had died in childbirth. Although the two families had known each other for years, it is said that Lucy's family disapproved of Harold.

Not long after the war, the Bostons moved to Cheshire so that Harold could take care of the family tanning business. They set up home in the village of Norton, a few miles from Runcorn, and within sight of Norton Priory, an extensive monastic site with remains dating back to the twelfth century. These made a lasting impression on Lucy. The Priory's most celebrated feature, a fourteenth century colossal statue of St. Christopher carrying the infant Christ, makes an important and mystical appearance in *The Children of Green Knowe*. But the ancient site asserts its presence in her short stories too, and with its lake and crumbling house built over ancient abbey ruins (and demolished in 1928), Norton Priory surely provided the model for Abbey Manor in "Curfew".

The Aunt Catherine and Uncle Tom of the story—she with her passion for gardening, he with his hatred of pretentiousness and brusque sense of humour—are clearly based on Lucy and Harold. After Lucy's death, their son Peter (who would later illustrate the Green Knowe books) recalled his father's volatile temper in those days at Norton and an incident in the garden which found its way obliquely into "Curfew":

> He was intensely moved by music, painting and architecture, and ruthlessly intolerant of anything which he considered meretricious. The paintings of Alfred Munnings and Fortunato Matania would send him into an apoplectic rage; so did our loyal and devoted gardener when he was once rash enough to state that "no power on earth would shift" a certain stone which needed removal.

And like Uncle Tom and Aunt Catherine, the Bostons enjoyed gently unsettling the younger relatives who came to stay with them. After Lucy's death a nephew, Michael Hemming, recalled holidays in Norton, when "Uncle Thrash would come in with a *papier-mâché* wolf mask on his face to frighten us. Lucy would read us exciting stories from *The Master of Mysteries*[5] and other books. Sometimes there would be marvellous stories which she invented as she went along. She never lacked imagination."

It's likely then that at least some of the stories in this collection were made up for the entertainment of the teenage boys who stayed with the Bostons at their Cheshire home in the 1930s.

But, though Lucy found lasting creative inspiration at Norton, the wider environment was a source of vexation to her and Harold. Her Cheshire home, she later recalled

---

[5] Probably *A Master of Mysteries* (1898) by L. T. Meade and Robert Eustace, a series of stories recounting the adventures of the sceptical supernatural investigator John Bell. L. T. Meade was the pen name for Elizabeth Thomasina Meade Smith (1854-1914). She was also a prolific author of novels for children.

wistfully, was "in a pocket of country depreciating rapidly under air pollution from Widnes. Its former hilly beauty showed ghostlike through, enough to feed imagination and melancholy in equal proportion." And imagination, melancholy and despair at increasing industrialisation combined to produce another strange tale, "Pollution".

Though it isn't specified, the setting is clearly Cheshire once more, and the factory-hating owner of the house where the narrator is employed is another manifestation of Harold Boston. Years later Peter Boston recalled how his father was engaged in "a constant baiting of ICI at Runcorn whose chimneys discharged smelly smoke over the area, leading to an ever increasing number of dead trees." Harold had special postcards printed which he regularly sent to the Chairman of Imperial Chemical Industries: "Further to my communication of [blank] I have *once again* to report that on [blank] the air was polluted by filthy stinks from your Runcorn factory . . . " But the rhetoric of Mr. Hunt in "Pollution" is even stronger: "They behave, with their smoke and slag heaps, as if they had killed the very forces of nature. But nature has a dual personality. They may think its beauty not worth bothering about, but it may still have surprises for them more hideous than they expect."

A revulsion at pollution and the galloping pace of modern life never left Boston either. She was eighty when she delivered the following speech at a college in Reading in May 1972, but she might as well have been addressing the 1933 Runcorn Chamber of Commerce: "Development is always the most boring standardisation, the obliteration of a personal creation and imagination. Pollution is not only of the air and the water and the land, and insecticide and weed killers do not only destroy the birds and wild flowers; they shrivel and pollute the mind also."

The Bostons separated in 1935 and Lucy left Cheshire with her son to travel in Italy and Austria where she trained as a painter. She returned to England in 1937 when Peter went up to King's College, Cambridge, and in 1939 she bought the moated old Manor House in the Cambridgeshire village of Hemingford Grey. This was to be her home and source of inspiration for the rest of her life.

A picture, painted by William Garden Fraser in 1899 and partially reproduced on the boards of this book, gives a reasonable idea of the state of the house when Boston first acquired it. The view is from a footpath along a bend in the River Great Ouse; we're looking from the north-west, at a Georgian brick façade, originally part of a much larger, rectangular structure that was partly destroyed by a fire in 1798. What allowed much of the main building to survive the blaze is not visible in the painting. In fact you only really get hints of it when you walk round the back of the property, where you see weathered stonework around arched windows. For the Georgian brickwork was wrapped around a twelfth century Norman Hall, with walls of Barnack stone three feet thick. And it was this ancient core that Boston set about exposing and restoring.

The change of scene and sheer amount of hard work that the restoration entailed may well have provided a welcome focus after the breakdown of her marriage. But perhaps more importantly Hemingford Grey and its ancient Manor provided Boston with a haven from the noise pollution she so hated. *Memory in a House*, in which she describes her life in The Manor, opens with a paean to the quietness of rural England in the first half of the twentieth century—the "primeval silence" that attracted her to Hemingford Grey in the first place—and a lament for its passing: "Pockets of divine silence still exist in blissful distant places," she writes. "Their fascination is in the maintenance of what was a condition from the beginning of life, a natural beauty so taken for granted as to be unrecognised until it had gone. The present generation has no conception of silence. If it could be imagined it would be the silence of death, not of abounding life. Formerly it enfolded everything. We broke into it and it closed around us again. This gave great interest to sounds when they occurred, lost now since noise is the continuum . . . "

"The Tiger-Skin Rug" was written some years before she bought The Manor, but it's hard not to think of the old house surrounded by its magnificent garden when reading the story today. And it's a story in which silence, or rather the breaking of it, is used to chilling effect.

A succession of noises, some familiar, others entirely foreign to their setting, herald the supernatural intrusion and the story's catastrophe: the sound of a mechanical organ, the malignant chattering of monkeys, the purring voice of the mysterious Dr. Sathanos, the hysterical yelping of a jackal, a mysterious nocturnal wailing, and a final, echoing gun shot.

And Boston is never better than when describing the jittery response of nature to the events of the story: "I heard the wood outside as restless as I: there seemed a perpetual rustle without enough wind to make it; birds would start twittering from their sleep here and there; a nearby jay woke me as I was dozing, then a rabbit screamed—poor little devil, I always hate to hear them—and every leaf outside the window seemed to itch."

Boston originally called this tale "An Asylum Story"— the idea being, perhaps, that its narrator is an inmate of a secure institution.[6] The theme of madness, the way the human mind can deteriorate under pressure, clearly inter-

---

[6] It was Philippa Pearce who gave it the title it was first published under, and this has been retained here.

ested her, and it recurs in "The Italian Desk" and "Blind Man's Buff". The manuscripts for these stories seem to date from the same time as "Curfew", "The Tiger-Skin Rug" and "Pollution", but the inspiration behind them or the particular occasions of their being written are lost to us. Boston never seems to have tried to have them published, and it's quite possible that they lay forgotten after the early 1930s, as she built a new life for herself in The Manor.

By the time *The Horned Man* was published by Faber and Faber in 1970, Boston was the highly-acclaimed, Carnegie Medal-winning author of half a dozen novels for children. The play has only ever been produced once, two years after its original publication, for a handful of performances by the pupils of St. Peter's School, Huntingdon to celebrate Boston's eightieth birthday. It certainly gives the impression of being aimed at a more juvenile audience than the stories, and it is, for me, less effective than either the tales in this volume or her longer children's novels. But the play does reflect Boston's lifelong dislike of religious bigotry and small-mindedness, and is most interesting, I think, when considered as a response to her own experiences of life on the edge of the Fens. For it wasn't only motor cars and aeroplanes that threatened the cherished silence along the banks of the Great Ouse—the hum of village gossip was never too far away, either.

Boston arrived in Hemingford Grey, unheralded, on the eve of the Second World War, an independent middle-aged woman with a son and no husband. She had bought and started single-handedly renovating a house which had stood long enough in the village for all sorts of supernatural rumours to have accrued around it. Furthermore she came to 1930s rural England after an extended stay in Italy and Austria and—stubbornly? naïvely? provocatively?—decided that she felt most comfortable wearing

Germanic national dress: "The *dirndl* is both practical and becoming," she later wrote. "I had been wearing it for three years in Cambridge without comment and continued quite naturally to do so. I never thought of it as other than my clothes. But Hemingford Grey . . . was more narrow minded than Cambridge."

Boston's contribution to the war effort was unique. Each week, beginning on 24 November 1941, she would invite young men from the nearby airbase at Wyton to gramophone record recitals in the old Norman Hall at The Manor, then, as now, known as the Music Room. And perched on makeshift benches made from old car seats, under beams that had been cut eight hundred years before, these WW2 airmen would close their eyes and listen to Chopin's ballads and Beethoven's concertos wound out on the magnificent old EMG gramophone.

But the steady stream of young men going in and out of the old haunted house owned by the independent, unattached woman who wore Austrian dress didn't go unnoticed. One day Boston opened the front door to find a senior-looking policeman on her doorstep: "He introduced himself with these surprising words—'Mrs. Boston? How do you do. When somebody is reported as a spy by every other person in their village, I think it is time the Chief Constable got to know her. May I come in?' " The misunderstanding was quickly cleared up, but one gets the impression that trust between the village and the resident of The Manor always had the potential for breaking down.

The treachery of the villains in *The Horned Man* is extreme and unmitigated, and Boston's contempt for religious intolerance and hypocrisy is clear. She was scarred perhaps by an overly strict religious upbringing; she later described the atmosphere in her childhood home as "rigidly, rabidly puritanical". But this did not entirely eradicate religious faith. There are moments of mystery in her fictions that owe something to the church—most notably the appearance of St. Christopher in *The Children of Green Knowe*, noted earlier. Boston described herself as "a near believer", and at some point in the 1950s she had carved on an ancient beam in the same Norman Hall, where she had entertained the WW2 airmen, a phrase coined by the Renaissance scholar Erasmus and later popularised by Carl Jung: *Vocatus atque non vocatus Deus adest*—"Whether called upon or not, God is here".

But if God was ever present in The Manor, so, Boston was convinced, were other invisible presences: "We all experienced considerable unease in the house at first," she admitted years later, "and inexplicable happenings continued for a good many years."

And, unsurprisingly, it was through sounds that these other presences were chiefly made manifest. This is the closest thing to a ghost story that Boston wrote in later life.

> One Sunday a young friend and I were weeding outside the front door of the supposedly empty house . . . We were bent, diligent and silent. After a while I said, "There seems to be too much going on in the house. I don't like it." Yes, she answered, she had been hearing it for some time. We took weapons before entering, I a hammer and she an iron bar—a measure of the unreasonable fear we felt in investigating a noise . . . There was nobody on the ground floor, but as we went upstairs a little hand bell rang in the Norman room. It was of course a bell I hadn't got. The place was unfit for furniture. We grimaced at each other and continued up. There was nobody on the upper floor.

"Well that's all right, isn't it? I think I'll go back into the garden," she said hastily. I would have gone with her, but the hand bell rang in the attic a short flight higher up. I went on into the expected but significant emptiness. This hand bell was to my hearing one of those genteel early Victorian things that stand on a table and are rung by twiddling a knob, in principle not unlike a bicycle bell. Could I have heard a distant bicycle through the unglazed windows? If so, why such a rush of panic? I have heard bicycle bells before.

As I reached the first floor on my way down, I heard a broomstick deliberately rattled down across the banisters of my new staircase. This is a sound that could not be made any other way, it is positive and unmistakeable. I yelled my friend's name— "Anne Rose! Don't play jokes on me." There was no answering laugh. "Anne Rose! Anne Rose!"

She was far away in the orchard and came running in answer to my shouts.

This incident is told for what it is worth, which is perhaps merely that my hair had stood on end in the proper manner. If something occurs outside what we call the natural order, its very smallness may be more immediately unnerving than, for instance, the eclipse of the sun to a tribe without astronomy, where holy awe must override any other feeling. Very small cracks in our outer shell of reason let in very cold air.

Another experience during one of her war-time concerts was more immediately spectacular perhaps, but less lastingly unsettling:

Towards the end of the war we acquired a new ghost. A late-comer was heard coming up the uncarpeted stairs to the music room door, outside which he waited for the record to end. When Elisabeth,7 as always, rose to open the door, every eye turned to see who was coming, but there was no one there. Thereafter this happened often, and in fact continued for some years after the war whenever I played to friends in the evening. We assumed it was the shadow memory, or haunting wish, of a lost airman. One evening just before the concert I received the news that one of our regulars had been killed. Half way through, steps were heard up to the door. Elizabeth opened it, and in came the dead man. Everybody froze and waited breathless to see him vanish. He was a small nervous man, and began to fidget under such fixed deadly staring. He looked anxiously around, adjusted his tie, his socks, but remained with us. Nobody liked to say anything. It was someone else, unknown to us but of the same name, who had been killed.

Lucy M. Boston died on 25 May 1990, but The Manor remains much as she left it.[8] Occasionally I perform the ghost stories of M. R. James by candlelight in the Music Room. And it feels entirely appropriate, in this place so rich with the past, so full of stories and storytellers and mysterious noises, to talk of animated bed-sheets and vengeful witches and children imperilled by magic. In

[7]   Elisabeth Vellacott, Boston's lifelong friend. She painted the image used in the dust jacket design of this book.
[8]   Boston's daughter-in-law Diana welcomes visitors by appointment; see www.greenknowe.co.uk. I cannot recommend a visit heartily enough.

her memoirs Boston talks of "the power" of the house, its mystery and her wish for its future—a wish that has, I think, been amply fulfilled: "It was," she writes, "and I hope still is, haunted and itself a haunter."

Robert Lloyd Parry
Great Eversden
Cambridgeshire
June 2011

Selected Bibliography

Yew Hall (London: Faber and Faber, 1954)

The Children of Green Knowe
  (London: Faber and Faber, 1954)

The Chimneys of Green Knowe
  (London: Faber and Faber, 1958)

The River at Green Knowe
  (London: Faber and Faber, 1959)

A Stranger at Green Knowe
  (London: Faber and Faber, 1961)

An Enemy at Green Knowe
  (London: Faber and Faber, 1964)

The Castle of Yew (London: Bodley Head, 1965)

The Sea Egg (London: Faber and Faber, 1967)

The House that Grew (London: Faber and Faber, 1969)

Persephone (London: Collins, 1969)

The Horned Man (London: Faber and Faber, 1970)

Nothing Said (London: Faber and Faber, 1971)

Memory in a House (London: Bodley Head, 1973)

The Fossil Snake (London: Bodley Head, 1973)

The Guardians of the House
  (London: Faber and Faber, 1974)

The Stones of Greene Knowe
  (London: Bodley Head, 1976)

Perverse and Foolish: A Memoir of Childhood and Youth
  (London: Bodley Head, 1979)

Curfew

Curfew

While my two brothers and I were at a preparatory school our parents were living abroad, so that we had to spend our holidays with relatives.

Our favourite uncle and aunt had bought a farmhouse on the outlying land of an old manor, of which the estate was being broken up. The big house, Abbey Manor, was being allowed to fall down in its own good time, the owner living in a small dower house in the park.

The cottage which Uncle Tom and Aunt Catherine bought had also been empty for a long time. Nettles grew up to the front door and even between the flagstones in the larder. The cottage however had been well built, with stone mullions, leaded windows and tiled floors. It had escaped the wanton smashing up that is the fate of most empty houses, perhaps because of its isolation. A profound silence brooded over it and the acres that went with it.

My Aunt had a passion for gardening, and there was much to be done before this weed-infested land should be disciplined to her intentions, but the wildness was a paradise for children.

Walks in the adjacent park were among the excitements of our visits. There was the empty Manor with its staring windows and lost melancholy garden, its weedy paths leading to locked gates. We had Sir Roger's permission to wander there, but never climbed the gate without a thrill, or chill, of expectation. One wing of the fifteenth century Manor had, with sacrilegious defiance, been built over the former Abbey graveyard. Here and there in the grounds, lying open among the rhododendrons were the empty stone coffins of forgotten Abbots, left there perhaps as being too heavy to carry away, or out of boastfulness. They were grand things, hand-hewn from solid blocks of local stone hollowed to the austerest outline of the human body with a round resting place for the head. We passed them with great awe and even with a kind of affection, as noble things treated with contempt and now part of our private landscape.

There was also a lake, reflecting the house and the stables, which were dusty, echoing and forlorn. Uncle Tom, who liked everything ship-shape, used to sigh over all this decay, but his wife had an eye open for everything that could be moved, bought, or made use of, such as a small wrought-iron gate, a sundial, or even, in an ambitious moment, as we all stood looking up at it, the little bell tower on the stables. Its four open arches and lead dome had the beauty of extreme simplicity against the pale green sky. "Why should it rot here?" she said. "It would suit our yard just as well;" but the yard, surrounded by fine old barns, was Uncle's special domain and he resented intrusion. "Rubbish," he said, "it's sure to be rotten. Besides I hate pretentiousness."

On our first visit to their farmhouse Aunt Catherine had been busy making a wild garden out of an acre or two of heather and stone. It was boggy in places and we helped to make water courses for her, while she laid stepping stones and contrived rough slab bridges. There was a high mound in the middle of this patch, apparently artificial, though of some age, judging by the hawthorn tree that grew on it, and it was crowned by a large boulder. In the course of her construction Aunt Catherine needed soil to raise her beds above the level of the surrounding damp, and, resourceful woman, looking at this hillock, decided to shift the top. With what delight we responded to her invitations to see if we could roll the boulder off; but our efforts were in vain. In the end it took a team of all hands, with levers, under the personal command of Uncle in his most arbitrary mood, to dislodge it. But at last the slope took possession of it and away it rolled on a clumsy and fortuitous course and came to rest at the edge of one of our little boggy streams. "Perfect," said Aunt Catherine by way of thanks and dismissal.

When next we came to stay, already her heather garden was taking shape. She had perfectly preserved the wild atmosphere, and the hillock was down almost to the level of the rest.

"Look, boys," she said, "we struck on this yesterday." She showed us the top of a trough or coffer of stone which her digging had half uncovered. The slab over it that had served as a lid had been prised up and now rested sideways, leaving a gaping hole through which the loose earth on top had poured in.

Aunt Catherine stopped with a gasp.

"When did you open it?" she asked Uncle.

"I haven't touched it, my dear."

"Then who has been here, and why?"

Was it a burglar? Was it treasure? We were all agog.

Aunt Catherine laughed uneasily and said she would guess that whatever was once in was now out, unless it was just old bones, and if so she was not going to disturb them.

"Old bones?" said Robert. "It's not the right shape for a coffin. Not like the Abbots'. There's no place for a head. Perhaps it was a criminal who had been beheaded. Or perhaps it was a case of 'Double him up, double him up' like Punch's victims."

"Or perhaps an animal Thing," suggested John hesitantly. He was young and imaginative.

Robert had been rather gingerly shovelling off the clay that still clung to the lid. "There are words on it," he said.

We all got busy with penknives, trowel and sticks to clean the letters.

Libera nos quaesimus Domine ab Malo.

Uncle Tom translated for us. "Deliver us O Lord from the Evil One."

"I don't like it," said Aunt Catherine. Then she shrugged and became practical again. "I'm short of a slab for my stepping stones," she said. "This will do very well. Come on, boys. All together, lift."

The slab took its useful place face downward in one of the paths, and the coffin itself was skilfully planted with bushes of rosemary and Spanish gorse and trailing rock-roses. By the time this story really begins it had a natural and undisturbed appearance, and around the wild garden that it dominated the lapwings and wagtails made themselves at home.

It was at the beginning of the long summer holidays. Aunt Catherine having completed one plan, was now looking for something new, and the suggestion of moving the bell tower from the Manor stables was raised again. We set off with Uncle Tom one afternoon to examine it. The Manor stables surrounded three sides of a courtyard and were in atrocious condition. The once beautiful and elaborate coach house let in the rain through a hole in the roof. The loose boxes were crumbling with dry rot. Our footsteps and voices rang intrusively as we did a tour of inspection before mounting the ladder to the lofts, and we explored such of these as had floors that would bear us. Spiders and rats were all that moved there now. Uncle Tom was the first to go up the second ladder and thrust his body as far as the knees into the little cupola, while Robert and John were jostling on the lower rungs, their heads level with the opening. I was alone on a little square landing; on one side of me was the ladder, on three were doors opening into dark lofts. We had already explored them and knew them to be empty, and therefore I was very scared to hear a hoarse burst of laughter rather like a horse's cough that seemed to come from one of them. I tugged at my brothers, and they came down, including Uncle who had finished his measuring and tapping. I told them there was someone there, and we all went round again, and I am afraid I took care neither to be first nor last, in or out, of any of the rooms. But we saw nothing and I was mercilessly teased for my fear as we returned home.

At supper that night my Aunt heard all about it. The measurements were very suitable, the condition not bad—"Though the bell's missing," said Uncle Tom; "You get a splendid view of our place from the roof, Catherine; I could see your Bad Man's coffin quite plainly. There's the chap that heard him too," he added, pointing his fork at me. "Made us all feel quite queer. I'll go and see Sir Roger tomorrow. They say he'd sell the hat off his head if he could. I like the idea of having a bit of the old house here. Anything new looks new."

"Don't you bring anything too old over from the Manor," said Aunt Catherine; "leave the ghosts behind anyway."

"It's too late to warn me about that," he retorted. "It was you who took the lid off the Bad Man's coffin."

"It was open already."

"Well, who rolled the boulder away that was supposed to keep him down?" and again he pointed at us with his fork, and we grinned, though shudders ran down our spines.

The next day Sir Roger himself happened to pass our gate. He stopped to speak to us all, even Robert, John and me, grimy and barefoot as we were.

"You are digging yourselves in very nicely here, I must say," he said to Uncle. "It all looks very jolly. I like the way you do it, too. Of course I have no choice but to sell what I can, but these gimcrack buildings do gall me."

This was a good opening, and before long bargaining for the bell tower had begun. It ended in Uncle's favour, because at the last moment he brought out his trump card—there was no bell.

"But there being no bell is one of its greatest attractions," said Sir Roger. "There's a legend, you know. It was called the Judas bell, but where it originally came from and who betrayed what I don't know. It was the old curfew, and of course if people are out when they ought to be in, things are likely to happen to them. The old people round here say the bell had a 'familiar'. The last person who rang it was my great grandfather, who did it for a wager. And it is a fact that he was found dead. Rather horribly dead. After that the bell was taken down and destroyed."

"Well, you can't expect me to buy a legend about a bell that is missing," said Uncle Tom, and the bargain was settled at a very small figure.

Before the end of the holidays the graceful little bell tower was set up on the middle building in our stableyard. Both Uncle and Aunt were pleased. It was repainted to match its new position and looked well there.

Wet weather had set in. We had grown tired of all the games that can be played in the house. Then Robert said he would go and fish in the Manor brook and we followed with jam jars of worms. We had to cross the wild garden, which had, since Uncle's jokes, begun to stir sinister feelings in us. The lapwings cried and veered and flung themselves along the wind, the thin rain pattered in the little brown streams, and the wagtails looked sharply at us, and ran hither and thither as though disguising their real activities. We began to run, and shooed them away as if they were unwanted thoughts, but as we paused half-way across the stile into the park and looked back, there they all were as before, and the curlews sounded derisive as if we had no business there. The little stream through the park had invaded the grass at its edge beyond the cast of Thomas's 10/6d fishing rod, and the lake into which it flowed had swollen into damaging proportions. The cinder road that led to the Manor farm was under water, and the farmer was there with Sir Roger, bitterly complaining that it was all because the outlet sluice was blocked and had never been mended, and that the lake itself was silting up and so full of weeds you couldn't tell where it began and where it ended. Sir Roger was listening with a pained expression. He promised to have it seen to as soon as the flood subsided enough to allow work to begin. As for us, we spent the afternoon happily testing the depth of every overflow and returned home wet to the skin.

A week later dredging operations began on the lake. The sluice was opened and the water sank to mud level. The weeds were cut down, and a band of old men in waders were wheeling the smelly fibrous mud in barrows along planks. We were there of course to watch. Much came to light that would never have been expected. A sunken boat, a scythe blade, a weather vane, a skull, and most surprising of all, a bell. It was of unusual shape, but covered thickly with sharp flakes of rust. The pivot of its tongue was rusted up solid so that it could not swing.

"It's the old Judas bell like enough," said one old man. "Didn't I hear tell that your Uncle had bought the bell tower? That's an odd thing for anyone to buy. I'd like to hear what my old woman would say if I came back one day and said I'd bought her a bell tower."

We ran back to announce the find at home, and Uncle Tom called for Sir Roger and took him along to look at it. Uncle had a flair for antiques, and he thought that the bell might prove to be incised in some pattern which might be curious or of interest. But Sir Roger was interested in nothing but "Sherry and whippets", as we knew from Uncle's indiscreet conversation. "Look at the rust on it," he said, "I can't take any money for a thing like that. Certainly, do what you like with it. I'm not superstitious, but I wouldn't touch it."

Uncle shook his head at me and said we must expect the worst.

The bell was sent away to be cleaned and repaired, but even in its absence we now had a prickly feeling of foreboding. I remember the golden September weather, the scent of southern wood and lavender, and the yellow leaves spotted with black that were beginning to fall. But for us the garden had become haunted. We no longer basked in it quite at our ease, or felt as heretofore that earth and fields, trees and sky were all our own. There were darker corners where we definitely did not go, where in a game of "I spy", for instance, nobody thought of hiding or looking.

It was on the last morning of the holidays that the bell came back. It was delivered by van, wrapped in sacking, with its now mobile tongue thickly wedged and muffled in felt. We all hung around while Uncle unwrapped it. Seeing us so deeply interested, he made quite a ritual of it, marching off to the barn with us in procession behind him. The clapper he had kept muffled till the last. It was to be "unveiled". When at last he pulled the first toll the sound that it gave out was so unexpected as to be quite shocking. It was a high wide-carrying note, and though it had a certain churchiness, there was in it something wild and almost screamlike. The afternote that vibrated long after within the bell sent a creeping chill up my spine. When the last sinister tingle had faded out of the shaken air, Aunt Catherine said, "I'm certainly not going to have *that* rung for dinner. It would take away my appetite." Uncle seemed not disposed to dispute it. He said, "If they rang that at curfew, they gave you fair warning."

We were to go back to school the next day, and this was a thought that blotted out all others. It was important to get the most out of the last afternoon. Towards sunset when we were playing "I spy", I was crouching in a deep clump of red dogwood, not far from the house, holding my panting breath and listening for the approach of Robert and John. I heard their voices drawing off in the wrong direction, and was beginning to feel I had time to straighten my stiff knees before they could possibly return, and then to hope they wouldn't be too long, when with no other warning a feeling of utter isolation and panic took me. I felt I was deserted, exposed to unknown dangers, perhaps trapped. I turned involuntarily to look behind me, and saw two long-nailed soily hands begin to part the leaves, and an evil face looked in. His hair and cheeks were clotted with earth, through which his yellow teeth showed more on one side than the other, his eye sockets were appallingly hollow, and he lifted his chin as the blind do when they seek.

I shot out of the bushes like a rabbit when the ferret looks in, and ran as hard as my legs would carry me to the house. My clamour soon brought Robert and John and Aunt Catherine, to whom I could give no better explanation than that I had seen a horrible face. She calmed me as best she could, saying it was probably a tramp coming in to pick up apples, and Uncle Tom should go round and send him off. Confidently she and Uncle exchanged that word as if it met the case perfectly—some tramps, a tramp, the tramp—as if a casual word like that could cover such lurking horror. Uncle Tom went striding off looking very fierce, but he came back having seen nobody.

Dusk had come. It was cold and the wind was rising, and we, as may be imagined, had no heart to play outside. So after tea Aunt Catherine let us light the fire, and we persuaded her and Uncle to stay with us and tell us ghost tales—the others I think out of pure love of sensation, and I because it was the only way that I could get company for my thoughts and persuade the grown-ups to talk, however insincerely, on the same subject. The session opened of course with a little lecture from Aunt Catherine about the folly of the whole thing. Then the curtains were drawn and Uncle Tom began. His personality and prestige added to the effect, for he was tall and bony and we held him in awe. He told the old stories about midnight coaches, about grinning lift-men who had been seen in a dream the night before, about grey monks who had passed people on the stairs and figures standing at midnight by one's bed; and they all to me had the same face.

The wind rose rapidly in accompaniment to his tales, and our feelings of horror were already far outstripping the merits of his invention, when a really terrible thing happened. A gust of wind tore open the casement and at the same time the bell in the tower gave a jerky ring. There was no need to tell us any more stories. Our hearts were tight with presentiment. Its variable sound came and went with the gusts even after the window was tightly closed again. It was not like a bell rung on purpose, but a bell evilly twitching on its own.

"This is quite intolerable," said Aunt Catherine. "No one will sleep a wink tonight if that goes on."

"Don't get in a fuss," said Uncle; "I'll go and take out the clapper. Nothing could be simpler. Now, boys, off to bed."

Up we went perforce, keeping close together, and clustered at our bedroom window to see him do this act of bravery. He seemed to waste hours talking to Aunt in the hall while we waited upstairs and listened to that vibrating shudder from the bell, the irregularity of which made it even more fraying to the nerves. The shadows under the yard walls were peopled for me with precise terror, and so was the room at my back. The keyhole howled too, and the wind in the chimney buffeted hollowly. At last we saw Uncle Tom come out into the light from the back door, and go down the yard where we could only by straining keep him in sight. Shadows swallowed him up and we heard the barn door slam behind him. We fixed our eyes on the outline of the bell tower, and again it seemed an age before we thought we could distinguish his head, shoulders and arms waving against the sky.

"There he is," said John, in a whisper. Uncle had seized the bell and the clanging stopped; but a moment later we heard him yell with the whole force of his great lungs, and his body disappeared down the man-hole. The bell stopped, but the wind still blew and it was hard to tell where sounds came from. Robert thought he heard a dog-fight going on somewhere. But Uncle Tom didn't come back. Time seemed too short now. We imagined how long it would be before he would appear, then doubled it, trebled it, and began again.

At last Aunt Catherine came out and shouted for him, ran half-way down the yard and shouted again. The maid came out too, and presently the yard was full of people with lamps and flash-lights. They went into the barn after Aunt Catherine, and came staggering out carrying some-one towards the house. We were seized with shame and undressed as quickly as we could, jumping into our beds. But Robert went on to the landing and called down the stairs to ask what had happened.

"Go to bed, boys, and for the Lord's sake keep quiet and keep out of the way," said a woman neighbour. "Your uncle has had a nasty accident."

And then we heard the horrible mad banshee sound of the maid having hysterics in the kitchen.

Pollution

I was in my first year at the Varsity and had taken the offer of a post as holiday tutor to a delicate boy. My em-
ployer, Mr. Hunt, was unknown to me and the district
on the map unpromising, though the name, St. Mark's
Abbey Lodge, suggested antiquity; but I wanted to earn
some pocket money, and as I usually get on easily with
most people, and am not, I flatter myself, in any way shy
or peculiar, I was not apprehensive.

As I approached in the train the country grew darker
with the smoke of chimneys. From the station where we
stopped at dusk the skyline was quite fantastic with their
tall shapes along the line of a river. Many masts too, and
the bulk of ships' funnels confused the outline on the sky.
It was early autumn and a mild quiet evening. I waited a
little while outside the station to see if anyone had been
sent to meet me. *Reaping the Whirlwind* confronted me in
huge letters on a cinema hoarding, and "Brutal Murder
of Nightwatchman" repeated itself annoyingly from the
posters of the local paper along the pavement. A swarm of
newsboys scrambled for the evening edition with coarse
guttural shouts. I called a taxi, and was relieved to learn
from the driver that my destination was some distance
outside the town; and on the way there I took my first
impression of the country. It was well wooded and had
obviously in earlier days had both character and beauty,
but it had that forlorn look of country already sold to

the town; it was doomed to be streets, and no one now tended the hedges. The cottages needed new roofs, their garden gates wanted hinges, as if their landlord already saw them swept away for road widening schemes. But as we climbed a hill and descended into a valley, slowing up towards the gates of an old-fashioned house, it seemed to me that already a more golden light lay over the corn-fields, and the low clouds moved across the valley with a more settled calm.

Mr. Hunt was at the front with a pair of shears trimming a yew peacock, of which there were several. He greeted me with consideration, though without a smile, and led me into the drawing room for a drink. I quickly guessed by the general appearance of the room, which, though large enough and comfortably furnished, was somewhat ne-glected, that there was no lady in the house. When he had poured me out a drink, and we exchanged the ordinary civilities of introduction and welcome, Mr. Hunt stepped out into the hall and called rather sharply for his grand-son. He apologised to me for leaving me again so soon, saying he had his work to finish.

I realised that I was not going to have much company, but at least was not to be afflicted with a chatterbox. I heard a hesitating rather dragging step on the stairs, and Mr. Hunt saying, "Mr. Gable is here, go in and be polite. You should have been waiting." So this was to be my charge.

He came in cautiously, prepared, as children are when they meet grown-ups, for any degree of difficulty, embar-rassment, bad temper or peculiarity, and any size or shape. He seemed relieved, and so was I, for he looked compan-ionable, and we shook hands on it. He was a small fair boy with one thin leg in irons. He did the honours of the house quite well and showed me to my bedroom.

The whole house was a pleasant surprise, beautifully simple and rural, and my bedroom pleased me particularly. It contained almost no furniture but a large curtained bed, some chairs, and a writing table, but there was a dressing room, too, and both had pleasant aspects. David hung half out of the low wide lattice in the bedroom and drew my attention to a large flowering shrub underneath which he said was a good magnet for all kinds of "bugs". He collected them, it seemed, and I came and looked over his shoulder. The walls of the house were covered with stout old pear trees. David told me that the gardener, who was very fat, had climbed in that way the day before when the lock had stuck in the door, and had to be picked from inside. He showed me a bush with a red admiral poised on it, and I looked across the garden and lane to a farm yard opposite with a large pond in the middle of the cobbles where cattle were drinking. Open country surrounded the house intersected by canals, and every field seemed to have its pit or hollow full of water. David and I hung out of all the windows in turn while he showed me the landmarks. The Hunts' estate, recently purchased, was not large, but everywhere well kept, the white gates clean and well painted, the hedges layered, and several spinneys of new trees growing up.

At dinner that night I learnt more of my host. David, who till then had chatted easily, now became as dumb as a bell without a clapper. I myself am usually an easy talker, regarding it as a social duty, but I soon ceased to make the effort as I saw a slight frown of coldness on Mr. Hunt's face if he had to listen to any sentence of no particular value.

He himself spoke seldom and abruptly, but he referred to his estate with pride, saying that it was time somebody resisted the encroachments of the town. The country had been beautiful from the earliest ages until now and it was to be his life's work to put the clock back, as he expressed it, in that small area, hoping to increase his influence as his wealth might allow. The smoke nuisance was to him as a red rag to a bull, and anyone who rashly mentioned it at the dinner table, as I learnt to my cost, laid himself open to the sharpest retorts, and was a victim for all the venom that the old gentleman felt against the factory owners. But he would talk sometimes, as elderly people do, in a high-flown strain about the old times, ending in an invective against modern men, who, he said, were as rapacious as thieves, spared nothing that could be put to their own use, and spread a blight wherever they settled. "They behave, with their smoke and slag heaps, as if they had killed the very forces of nature. But nature has a dual personality. They may think its beauty not worth bothering about, but it may still have surprises for them more hideous than they expect." After these words we all lapsed into total silence; they lingered in my head as we sat round the table with the candle flames gently swaying, and stuck in my memory as odd sentences sometimes do.

I have had reason since to think of them as being ominous. As I slept that night in my big comfortable bed, with the leaves of the pear trees rustling round the windows, the scattered phrases of the day furnished me with an unpleasant dream about the old times, and the dark forces of the earth, which took the form of octopus-like creatures heaving up out of slag-heaps, and obscurely predatory. It is a common-place that one sleeps uneasily in strange beds, and so in spite of a bad night I rose cheerfully the next day.

After the morning's work, at which I found that I had a very intelligent pupil, David and I went for a walk. I was interested in an immense round tower that crowned the rising ground a few hundred yards from the house. It was built in good Roman style of blocks of sandstone and very massive. Huge round arches opened in the sides, and there was a Latin inscription carved all round the top which served as an extra Latin exercise for David and me as we walked round the outside deciphering *Haec aqua de cambriae montibus derivata est* and more of the same sort, ending, it is true, with the disappointing date 1872. "The year," David commented, "that grandfather was born. It is the St. Mark's Water Tower. Those huge iron pipes inside are the mains, two up and two down; they are the same as these," he added, going towards some sections of pipes ranged on the ground round us; formidable iron tunnels, big enough for David to walk through, and myself too if I crouched somewhat. I was impressed with the thought of that volume of water constantly flowing up and down *De cambriae montibus* as the motto said.

I liked the direct connections with the Welsh Hills. At the foot of the tower was a farm which we passed through as we made our way on. We walked to the site of St. Mark's Abbey which gave its name to the district, and got home for a quiet tea. David and I got on well together. He was a likeable boy, apparently lonely with his somewhat severe grandfather, and the "bug" collecting was a hobby in common for us.

I found that I was to have my evenings very much to myself. Mr. Hunt was often out seeing to this and that on the estate. The place began to take hold of my imagination as I shaded the match with my hand to light the many candles—(for they had not yet installed electric light in the hamlet of which ours was the biggest house). Outside in the half light the flowers were beginning to look sodden and faded, the leaves yellowing, and the last sheaves being taken away by a late-working team of men and horses. The harvest moon was up, and breathing the sweet country smells I had that haunting feeling of autumn more acutely than I ever remember, as if the earth in its cycle were turning away from day into night, from summer into winter, from youth into age and from civilisation back into those dire and mysterious dark ages. I gave an involuntary shudder; it was cold anyway, and I closed the French windows and went in to read. There was no wireless to keep one in touch with the vulgar humdrum world, but a good selection of books chiefly of the sixteenth and seventeenth centuries.

One day I had sent David up to wash his hands, as I cannot believe anyone can do a neat Latin exercise if his hands or hair are slovenly. I was taking the opportunity of his absence to look up "spawn" which happened to be the next word in his unseen, which I did not know myself. My finger was tracing down the S's when I heard a loud scream from upstairs. David was shouting for me at the top of his voice. I ran up to join him, thinking he must have met with some accident, but he met me on the landing, seized my arm, and trembling with excitement dragged me into the bathroom. "It came out of the tap and fell into my hand," he said, pointing to the basin where I saw one of the most revolting insects that could be imagined. David was obviously terrified of it, though normally not at all squeamish, and I had always considered myself quite a fair entomologist; but this was something I could not place at all. Its soft and active body was carried on tentacle-like limbs, which gave it a look of menace and rapid manoeuvring; its head terminated in a sucker like the nozzle of a vacuum, and its protuberant eyes had a definite expression.

This sickening creature was turning slowly round on the slippery porcelain, and I had instantly only one thought, and that was to despatch it, which I did with the nearest weapon, and afterwards felt quite sick, for I thought it had squeaked. I tried to cover up the violent impression it had made on me by apologising to David, whose eyes looked twice their usual size, for having so thoughtlessly killed what must have been a most interesting specimen for his collection, but actually nothing would have induced me to touch the thing. We turned on the tap and the horrid remains were carried down the drain.

After this incident the bug collection went rather out of favour. If we had even pretended any enthusiasm for it we must have searched for another of these interesting specimens, whereas actually we both were secretly nervous lest under sponges in the house or stones in the garden we might accidentally find one.

We therefore turned our attention to fishing and decided to explore those pits which were so common in the fields. We fished for the whole of one sultry afternoon without any sort of a bite. Our supply of maggots was nearly exhausted when with cries of excitement David caught a minnow very flashing and lively for its size. I myself had done little or no fishing, but I felt it was my *rôle* as tutor to show some knowledge and initiative, so I suggested we should use the live minnow as bait for possible pike. This we fixed up, and David cast his line with renewed interest. He was rewarded almost immediately by a sharp tug, and jerked up his rod. There was no pike on the line, but as I caught the gut and glanced at the minnow, already quite inert, I saw with a shock of disgust that it had one of those suckers attached to its side and already swelling with its meal. This was slightly larger than the first we had seen, and fell back without my touching it into the pond with a plop like an egg. I did not know if David had seen what it was. He made no comment, and we left the pond by mutual consent, on the excuse that it was tea time. I was ashamed of myself for my extreme unreasonable shrinking from these creatures, and for my sympathy for David when he said airily at bedtime that he didn't need a bath tonight, and when later I went into his room to see if his light was out, I didn't really think it funny that he had pushed corks up the taps and put the plug in the plug hole, nor did I show that I had noticed. After all, a child is very impressionable, and often minds intensely even a spider. I can remember in my own childhood being terrified out of sleep by being shown a dead tarantula in a glass case. But this beast conjured to mind all that was loathsome in jungle or swamp.

The papers next morning had an article that caught Mr. Hunt's attention. He began reading with his mouth full—a bad fault in children, but old men, I thought, often do it on purpose as if to say, "I am so busy and my business is so important, I must do two things at once." So I missed the opening words, but presently gathered that the subject was water pollution. "Various households have complained to the Water Company of foul insects coming from the taps, also of an unpleasant smell in the water." ("I noticed it myself this morning," interpolated Mr. Hunt.) "The local sanitary inspector is of the opinion that the creatures are an unusual form of larvae of the *Scarabaeus surculus maximus*, certainly of an abnormal size, and he supposes there must be some carrion in one of the company's reservoirs which has attracted them. This, of course, will be immediately investigated, and in the meantime householders are advised to boil any water used for drinking purposes, to despatch the larvae wherever found."

This article was the first of a series. Every day somebody wrote a letter on the subject. Mr. Hunt sent one suggesting that the smell in the water could be traced to the carelessness of some local chemical works. Others suggested that the blood suckers, as they had come popularly to be called, had come over in some foreign cargo boat; others again that they were British insects and quite harmless. An indignant Colonel wrote saying that he had been seized on the fingers by one no less than four inches long, and that he had difficulty in dislodging it; a later edition announced his serious condition. A Methodist minister of unusual acumen reminded us of "Spawn of Satan" and that there was Scriptural authority for the belief in their existence.

About this time too, the headlines were devoted to a sequence of atrocious midnight murders in the neighbouring manufacturing town, a place so dismal, grimy and degenerate as naturally to breed crime. It was easy to imagine the killer skirting the dark side of tall buildings and lying in wait for his victims in the gloom of some back alley. The circumstances of the deaths were as mysterious as revolting, and the police were at a loss. But no papers were discussed at St. Mark's Abbey Lodge. Mr. Hunt had a frigid objection to sensationalism or even excitement. However, when ultimately the Home Office sent a special representative, a certain well-known entomologist called Professor Bennet, to take charge of the Water Investigation Committee, Mr. Hunt offered him hospitality.

I was very glad to have a change of company, and of course interested to be now in touch with all investigations. For we had seen several more of the creatures, and I was getting into a nervous habit of looking out for them in every likely or unlikely place, for the later ones were larger, and seemed able to leave the water for longer periods, so that one looked in all corners of the bathroom before getting into the bath, and once I saw something disappear under the woodwork of the bath, and could not be sure if it was a mouse or not. I confess they were getting on my nerves. The old gentleman, too, was getting peevish and unreasonable. The Professor's arrival was very welcome to us both.

He was a learned-looking man with a high imposing head, but he was jovial and sensible and quite without any self-importance. On the evening of his arrival we had the first really sociable dinner since I had been there. Everybody talked, even David. I heard now from the Professor the history of the Water Tower. Through it, he said, passed the water supply for the whole urban area. It was a great feat of engineering, and in order to make the lake that supplied it they had had to evacuate a whole valley of its sparse population. It had then been dammed across and slowly flooded by the streams from all the hills around, the sources of the main river. He told me too that in flooding this valley they had swept away a lot of local superstitions, for there was a deserted quarry village on the bleak hillside, whose inhabitants had all left for an unknown cause, apparently in the early sixteenth century, for there were no houses in it at a later date than that, though some of them had date stones of 1517. The quarry, which was disused and waterlogged, was said by the Welsh peasants to contain a bottomless pit, and no sheep would pasture near it. "The Welsh," he added contemptuously, "are a perverted superstitious race."

He was to analyse the water and examine the valves the next day and courteously invited me to accompany him. "Though if," he continued, "as people here seem to expect, we find the Eternal Worm himself writhing in his slime, I am afraid my education will prove to have been inadequate."

"Take the parson with you," piped up David, bouncing in his chair.

We all laughed, for the local parson was a bye-word. The Professor's solid scientific outlook and quasi-humorous smile were a pleasure and relief to me, and encouraged David to a bolder attitude. From his present gaiety and flushed cheeks I began to guess how much childish horror he had been suppressing in order not to forfeit my good opinion.

We now began to vie with each other in descriptions of the exact beastliness of the larvae, and David became quite hysterical, laughing about nothing, till he was sharply rebuked by his grandfather and ordered to bed. We three then spent a pleasant evening. Mr. Hunt was positively expansive, called me "my dear fellow", handed cigars all round, and Professor Bennet's interesting conversation kept us well entertained till the early hours.

Alas, the next morning brought us nasty news. There had been a sudden stampede among the sheep at a farm not far distant, while they were watering at the yard troughs, and one of them had fallen with its head under water, struggling violently, and a blood sucker the size of a cat was found on its throat. That was what we were told by the gardener; doubtless the tale had grown in the telling, and would grow still more. There is no limit to ignorant credulity. But it chilled the imagination. The servants talked, and from this time on, David would never willingly leave me.

However, I set him some work, drawing, because that was what he liked best, while I went with Professor Bennet to the Tower. He was more silent and thoughtful than on the previous night, and he tapped impatiently with his stick as he walked. We approached the iron gates without any conversation but mere civilities, and not even those as we came into the shadow of the structure.

The Tower Keeper came out from his little house to open the great oak doors. He was a tall stooping man with spare yellow hair and furtive eyes. He had the look of a dilapidated gentleman, and the bottle suggested itself as a probability. He looked an uneasy man, too, his face lined with worry, and he glanced quickly inside as he swung the doors back. It was high, hollow and dim, and against the great arched windows the air was seen thick with dust as if it were slightly foggy, and Professor Bennet and I sniffed the dank smell with suspicion and nausea. There was definitely something not right.

The Professor turned enquiringly to the Keeper, who seemed to understand the unspoken question, for he replied, "Sometimes more, sometimes less." I went in, while they paused on the threshold and talked for a while about the valves. I did not pay much attention as it seemed a purely technical discussion, but I understood that Bennet instructed him to close the incoming valves entirely and let the tank stand empty until further notice. Meanwhile I looked around at the mains like four great pillars going up to the roof which I knew constituted the tank and the dusty iron staircase that wound up between them. Only now I realised that there was no machinery. The water rose to that dizzy height by its own pressure.

The silence was oppressive, the voices at the door seemed to come from another world, and when at last they came inside, and Professor Bennet rapped on one of the pipes with his stick, the clang was monstrous in its reverberations, like the vast exaggerated unreality the present sometimes assumes when it breaks into our dreams, and in the instant of waking us feels as though it has split the atom.

He apologised for the noise, but added that at least he had scared no birds; the place seemed to have no living inhabitant, though several nests and piles of bird droppings showed that normally sparrows at least would have been found there. My gaze was travelling round the huge and dim interior as I made this observation, and my attention was engaged by such a strange impression of age and desolation, that though I did indeed notice it, I failed to attach any importance to the start that the Tower Keeper gave when the Professor remarked, "If this were in some other part of the globe, what a place for snakes!" The man came a step nearer and looking round began to speak in the confidential voice of a trusted servant who will not acknowledge a professional secret until it is first referred to by his superiors. "No, sir," he said, clearing his voice which had grown husky. "*Not snakes.*" He said this with such significance that Professor Bennet found no sense in it. He looked politely puzzled, and asked him to repeat it. But the Keeper had shrunk back into his manner of suspicious reserve, and his treatment of Professor Bennet was from this moment less deferential and even a little wary; he answered his questions, showed him the temperature and level gauges and the pressure dials, but it seemed as though the return to these technicalities, and the ordinary routine of the Water Company, had in some way disappointed him. He left us as we began to climb the winding stair. After six or seven revolutions we came high enough to see through the arches, and I commented on the change that the landscape seemed to undergo when seen in a Roman frame. My voice jarred on me and I stopped speaking. I had the feeling that my own accents, as they echoed down from the roof and wandered round the hollow structure, had changed in tone. They were shuddering and abrupt, as if some part of me were at large up there, and exposed to some invisible danger.

A cloud travelled across the sun at this moment, throwing the outer world into shade, and the floor of the Tower, now so far below us, into a grey dusk. There was a wind too as one climbed higher, flying through the arches in gusts that made us cling to the sides. At last we reached a small platform commanding the tank, which was open to the sky and filled with cold and colourless water. The surface seemed to me to give a slight heave as we looked in; that immediately subsided, and an icy metallic lapping of water was the only movement. I heard my voice saying to Professor Bennet—"Didn't you see the water move then?" He answered gravely, "I think that would be caused by the Keeper closing the valves. The underwater pressure would fall of course." He made several observations in his notebook, but told me it was useless to test the deposit till it had lain dormant for twenty-four hours at least, and we went down again, rather quickly, for we were very cold and anxious to reach the warm and sheltered earth.

Outside the Keeper was standing looking up at the crenellated edge of the Tower; the wan light fell full on his upturned face on which stood beads of perspiration, though apparently he was deep in thought. "You've closed the pressure?" asked Bennet. "Not yet, sir," replied the man, "I must give the other stations five hours' notice, but I'll do so as soon as possible." We hurried home without comment.

David's work was not well done. He had evidently not concentrated on it at all. "Could there," he said, not listening at all to my criticisms of his drawing, "at least, are there—I mean—" I waited, but he could not bring himself to finish his question. So I told him to sit up properly and to stop fidgeting, and we settled down to serious work together. I felt the need of it myself, and perhaps pushed the boy too far in my efforts to distract my own mind, for when we were interrupted by the gong, I saw that he looked quite ill. He seemed feverish, and we sent him to bed. In the evening, chiefly to prevent the maids coming in to him with their unwholesome gossip, I sat in his room pretending to read, but a prey to strange thoughts. Towards bedtime there was a knock at the door and the

Professor came in. He sat on the boy's bed and talked to us both for a while. He had said goodnight to Mr. Hunt who, he told me, puzzled that a new and noxious odour was reaching him when the wind was from the southwest, whereas the offending factory against which he was chiefly complaining lay to the northwest, had gone out in his car to investigate it, and might be away some time. David fell asleep to the sound of our voices, we finished our pipes in silence, and then wished each other goodnight, and I went to my own room.

The day had been long and gloomy, the cloud that had obscured the sun as we mounted the Tower had been the forerunner of many; rain had followed in sheets till all the view was dark and slimy. The window in my room rattled, and it was only by wedging it open to its widest that I could stop the incessant noise. In that position there was too much air for a wild night and the great bed curtains moved uneasily, but I hate a closed room, so there was no help for it. I put out the candle which smelt in the draught, and lay down with my large flash-light, a recent purchase, under my hand. I fell asleep after a while, and dreamt again that dream of my first night, but this time with an intensity of horror that I cannot describe. The long fumbling arms and yielding body of the monster pushed through the window and glided across the floor with a flop, and this flop, which I felt as one sometimes feels oneself drop in dreams, woke me up with my heart pounding. Against the drumming of the blood in my ears and the swish of the wind outside among the trees, I seemed to detect a sound along the floor, stealthy and trailing. I sat upright and turned on my flash-light. It lit the room brightly but unevenly, so I added the three candles that I had placed near my bed; but the sheets rustled so loudly as I moved to light them that after that I dared not move again, but sat, frozen like a stone, afraid to pull the blankets up lest under cover of that rustle another sound might occur unheard. I could see most of the room except the floor between the foot of my bed and the window. There was a pool on the window-sill into which the rain still faintly splashed, while the shadows in the corners seemed to leap like beasts held in leash, and the smoky stink of the waving candle flames blew past my nostrils. There was another smell, too, that sent me nearly crazy with fear. So there I sat with every nerve on edge for an age that seemed to have no connection with actual time, keeping watch on all I could see, with a space of terror below the bed and behind its bulging curtain that I could not watch. In this misery and in spite of all my vigilance, I must at last have dozed or half dozed, for I slipped into thinking that the wind that blew in at the window had the cold moaning quality of the wind on high moors and mountain tarns, and that the dwindling light of my flash-lamp on the walls was the light of the setting moon on the steep sides of a quarry. I felt that the Pit had yawned and Evil had come out of it. The candles were burnt out and the room was still, the shadows faint and steady, and now I saw it was the real dawn that was paling my lamp. The nauseating smell still lingered, but there was no sound but a distant barking of some large dog. My teeth were chattering and my knees knocking together, so I now plucked up enough courage to lie down in the bed, though craning my head all the while for any unusual sounds. If I relaxed and laid it on the pillows a moment it was only to start up again resting on my elbows and straining my ears. When after a while I did hear slow and stealthy steps approaching along the landing, and my door handle turned, I was in such a state that the last thing I thought of was an ordinary human being; and when the Professor came in wrapped in his dressing-gown, his hair rumpled into a point like a clown's on top of his head, and his green eyes small and blinking without his accustomed glasses, his reception must have shocked him; for I had scrambled up and was standing with my back to the head of the bed, half hidden by the side curtains, and holding my now exhausted flash-lamp above my head like a club. His nostrils dilated slightly and he looked anxiously at me as we sat down together on the bed. But I could find no words at all to describe my experience to him.

"What a night," he said. "I have not slept a wink. That boy tossed and talked in his sleep next door, and for myself my brain has been quite out of hand. What things one thinks of in the night! And that dog was the last straw. You evidently have been awake too. How would it be if we made some coffee?"

"You like plenty of fresh air, I must say," he went on, as I fought with the sleeve of my dressing gown. "The rain's run down in a pool under your bed."

I joined him by the window and we leant out together. The dawn was lowering and held no freshness. A few birds twittered restlessly as they do before thunder or an eclipse. Under my window was a litter of leaves newly torn off and several broken branches of pear smeared with mud. The Professor gave a long look at my face, and to my amazement I saw him make the Sign of the Cross.

We went down to the kitchen together and foraged in larder and cupboard. A homely sound of tins shaken to guess their contents—every type of light and heavy rattle, rice, sugar and macaroni, before the dull swish of coffee, or would it turn out to be moist sugar?—was soothing to my frayed nerves, and I talked quickly and senselessly like an excited girl, and made weak jokes about frying the milk. The Professor turned on the tap to fill the kettle, but no water came, having been turned off at the main by his instructions.

We were discussing which of the buckets was most likely to contain the drinking water, when there was a loud knocking at the front door, repeated a moment later with the clang of the front door bell. As we hesitatingly moved in that direction, the maids came out on the stairs in their nightgowns and overcoats as frightened as a pair of sheep.

Professor Bennet drew back the bolt and undid the chain, and as he paused before opening the door a loud and reassuring sniff was heard from the other side. He opened it, smiling wryly, and we saw one of the farm labourers from the tower farm standing there, unshaven and with his coat collar turned up round his dirty wisp of necktie. He looked furtively at us, rather defiantly, as if we were potential enemies, and said, "They want you to ring up the police and say there's been a murder at the Tower. T' Keeper's been done in. They say he went out to do his night round same as usual, and he's been found this morning as dead as an empty stocking."

We were all standing blankly considering this new calamity when old Mr. Hunt appeared. The maids scattered at once and began a busy clinking of pots and raking of the kitchen grate. The man was ordered to repeat his message, and I myself was chidden like a schoolboy, and told to ring up the police at once and not stand gossiping like an old woman. The labourer touched his cap and shuffled off, and the rest of us, though it was yet only six o'clock, separated to dress.

Breakfast was a difficult meal. Mr. Hunt looked at me with disfavour as I came down. I dare say I had black rings under my eyes. He greeted me shortly, and turned his attention to Professor Bennet. The Professor and I would have had much to say to each other if we had been alone, but Mr. Hunt was in a bad mood. He disputed everything we said, and constantly returned to his own theme—that it was a national disgrace if a man was to put up with a filthy stench in his own house and not be able to call anyone to account for it. He would sooner see the whole factory system blown up with all the people concerned in it. His grandchild, he said, was to get up and not be coddled. "And, by the way, Gable, I wish you would teach the boy to respect the garden—there's a disgraceful mess today under your bedroom window. He needn't smash down the trees to get his caterpillars."

I protested in favour of David, but he pooh-poohed me. His coffee was abominable; he was going to change the housemaid, a most irritating woman. Superstitious fool! Evidently something on his night journey had upset him very much, for he frowned heavily at his thoughts when not speaking.

"The farmers are as bad as anyone else," he went on, "they take no care at all. There was something at the side of the lane just by our gate as I came in last night. A horse or cow, I suppose, but the stink was specially bad just there, I had to put up the car windows and didn't see what it was."

To make matters worse the day grew darker instead of lighter, and before breakfast was finished we were obliged to ring for candles. It was clear that a severe storm was gathering; we lit our cigarettes and went into the garden to sum up the day's weather forecast. What wind there was was sudden and veering, and from every point of the horizon threatening clouds were closing in on us.

"It looks bad enough," said Professor Bennet, "but all the same I think I must go up to the Tower and carry out the analysis. That poor fellow's death does not make it any less pressing, and meanwhile we have cut off the water supply for half a county. I shall be glad if you will come with me."

My heart turned to lead. What I should have liked to do more than anything was to ring up a taxi and take the first train south. But I replied rather snappily, "Naturally."

As we passed the garden gate the first crackle of thunder tore the sky. It looked as if the whole volume of the storm had concentrated over the Tower which stood out as black as ink beneath it. We walked at a quick pace to hide our reluctance from ourselves, and to put on a good show before the country people, but when we got there the place was entirely deserted. They had removed the body to the farmhouse, where no doubt a crowd of neighbours was now gathered, and the police had examined the cottage and locked it up before they left. We had not expected this silence, and it was an added strain on my courage. I confess I could not bear the idea of going up the Tower again. But here was a most welcome hindrance, for we supposed the key to be locked in the cottage. We stood to shelter in its porch after we had ascertained that it was really deserted, and we looked at the Tower under its weight of storm. The clouds were brazen and jagged and every clap of thunder was preceded by a sound like the tearing of calico. The lightning seemed to hiss as it darted. I tried to imagine the reverberations of the thunder in that drum-like chamber, and I could guess how the wind at the top would seize on us like a malicious fiend and try to shake us off the stairs. And in the flickering livid shoots of lightning what might one not see?

I heard the Professor cry out, and turned to see him pointing and gazing, as previously the Keeper had done, towards the rim of the Tower, his face unrecognisable in its expression of horror; but at this moment a splitting and continuous zig-zag of lightning, simultaneous with a concussion of thunder as though the sky had fallen, made me put both hands to my head for fear of being blinded.

There followed an indescribable roaring and confusion, and peering through the torrents of rain that now beat on my face, and glued my eyelashes to my cheeks, I saw that the Tower had been struck. Sulphur fumes poured out of all its arches, and from inside came a pandemonium of noise as the great mains shot up columns of water that fell in a pounding waterfall on to the iron stairs, together with falling masonry, and the walls threw back a clamour of echoes magnified beyond the powers of hearing.

Witnessing this prodigious spectacle, I lost all sense of fear, and elated by excitement stood ejaculating to the Professor, whom I thought was at my elbow. The exterior of the Tower was still almost intact, but the tank was ripped open. I could see a great iron sheet hanging down in the centre and battered to and fro by the monstrous jet.

"Well, that should have settled it for us," I bawled, turning to the Professor, and taking a huge breath to relieve my feelings. But the Professor was a crumpled heap on the ground.

Water was squirting violently from the base of the Tower through the cracks and hinges of the big door, and I had to run through a surging lake to get help. I found two farm hands, and together we carried the Professor back to the house in a staggering splashing group. The storm seemed to have spent itself in that last stupendous burst, and now the sky was rapidly clearing; in spite of our burden a feeling of optimism grew in with the brightening air.

The Professor was not dead. He recovered consciousness that afternoon, but not his sight. He had two nurses in attendance, and no one was allowed to see him for several days. At last, however, they reported that his sight was returning, and I at my urgent request was allowed to visit him. He lay in the darkened room, and turned his head languidly to me, addressing me as if I were a total stranger.

This was a real grief to me, as I had developed a strong feeling of attachment to my companion in these dimly understood events, which I could confide in no one else with any hope of being believed. The only other witness, as I could not but suppose the Keeper to have been, was dead.

Actually Professor Bennet never recovered his memory of those last twenty-four hours, and the account which he ultimately wrote for the Home Office was a dry and uninteresting document enough, but satisfactory enough to all concerned, because after the Tower had been put right there were no further complaints; though I heard that there was some trouble among the men brought in to repair it, and that the first gang who went in after the water had drained away, came out within a quarter of an hour and decamped, leaving the place open behind them.

Blind Man's Buff

In the course of my profession I have listened to many strange confessions both true and imaginary, but I can remember none that seemed to give so much pain in the telling as this that I am putting on record. Every word seemed charged with difficulty and inhibitions, and it was only by using the greatest tact that I was able to gather even as much as I did. Even then I was at a loss how much to believe of it, though I usually pride myself on my quickness in seeing through a lie and tracing its motive. The usual rule is that the harder anything is to confess, the truer it is likely to be. For when anything touches a man very nearly, he is unwilling to speak of it. The glib confessor is romancing, either to increase his importance, or to cover something worse than what he actually owns up to. But what motives could a man have for making up those incidents in his story that Captain Fernley could not tell without a physical struggle? As he spoke he would alternately be faltering and bathed in sweat, or else he would rap it out at me as if he were afraid of being shouted down. He came to me as a patient in the most wretched condition, but even so his appearance was striking. In spite of the disfigurement of his heavy eye shade, I could see that he must have been an unusually handsome man, tall and graceful; and the full consciousness that he had of his outcast condition, could not eradicate from his manner the traces of a life of social success.

He was half-American, half-English; had been educated at Oxford and afterwards went into the American diplomatic service. It was easy to imagine him as a spoilt and brilliant young man with the world before him, though he told me little of that. What he seemed more ready to tell me was that he was no mere society dandy, but had a good athletic record and had made a name for himself while he was still at the Varsity as a mountaineer. He told me that at an early stage in his career he was sent out to Venezuela on some mission, and took the opportunity to do some climbing on the Sierra Nevada. These comparatively unknown peaks appealed to his ambitious nature more than the carefully charted Alps where almost every foothold is marked.

He took with him a native guide whom he chose, out of those who offered themselves, for his incomparable knowledge of the district, for his savage aboriginal appearance, and also partly for another reason less easy to advance. He had something in his glance, either of arrogance or hostility or secret power, that Fernley would not admit himself unwilling to meet. I have known men to buy a hunter for no other reason.

Perhaps something of his insolent, assumed mastery antagonised the Indian, or perhaps it was something deeper which no tact could have avoided. At any rate it was at this point that Captain Fernley began to get into difficulties and to flounder between sullen silences and agonised confidences.

The man Quibar had a natural grandeur of bearing and physique, and what it was that immediately jarred into being between him and the Captain I never fully learnt. Perhaps it was nothing but the action of one personality on the other, each of such a kind as to bring out unimagined depths of evil in the other.

I asked Fernley to tell me more about the Indian, and he said, making an effort to pull himself together, that he was a good guide, a silent man who never spoke unless spoken to and then only briefly. He was guide and self-appointed critic. In no sense was he a companion.

"He was a fiend," said Fernley, and to judge by his trembling he was not speaking loosely.

They climbed together for a week, roped in the closest collaboration, and Quibar tested the Captain's experience to its limit, and proved himself by far the better man. He was arrogant and impassive, and the Captain accepted every unspoken challenge, though, I gather, with growing anger. Here again the story broke down, and at this point could never be bridged.

"Quibar fell," the Captain almost shouted at me. He fell, damaging himself severely, and hung on to the rope which was round the spur of rock on which Fernley had barely foot-hold. He did all that mortal man could do to pull Quibar up. The guide was heavier than he, and there was a rock at his back which prevented him from getting into a position in which he could use all his strength. There was nothing to which he could attach the rope securely enough to hold while he went for help. Shouting was waste of breath, though he shouted like a trapped dog, and distant echoes howled it back. When he was utterly exhausted he remained chained to the rock by the rope from which Quibar—scornful, silent, and now hated—hung and watched him. All that night he endured it and the next day, struggling at intervals with ever less strength to haul up the rope. The bleak and terrible aspect of the wilderness of peaks around seemed to eat into his mind and poison it like a curse. He became delirious with sun and thirst and fear. The drop over which the rope hung was a hell he dared not see, but Quibar's eyes drew him like a magnet, and in spite of all the torture he must have been suffering, his harsh unspeaking lips wore a smile of triumph. To Fernley he came to signify all that was relentless and indifferent in their predicament. He was death incarnate, attacking not the life only, but the soul, with his insulting smile. Fernley took out his knife, and Quibar watched him as he severed the rope.

I believe that until he told me this, it had remained unconfessed on the Captain's conscience for twenty years. He looked indeed like a dead man, but continued his story from this point in a toneless voice. He had got back somehow to his camp, and collected a rescue party. In spite of fever and exhaustion he led them back to the scene of his dishonour, never doubting that Quibar was dead, and letting it be understood that the rope had frayed against the rock. He himself was lowered first over the cliff to locate the body, and however severely one must censure him for his loss of heroism, it is impossible not to sympathise with his horror when he found Quibar on a ledge of rock *alive*. A ghastly wound across his face had obliterated his eyes and his legs were useless, but on hearing Fernley's voice, his broken mask of a face was animated with hatred, and he attacked him with such ferocity that Fernley barely got away with his life, and had to send down two guides to take his place.

With a heart as heavy as sin and the thought of his future blackened by disgrace, he helped to haul the two guides and their burden to safety. Quibar had been exposed without food or drink, and with much loss of blood, for four days and nights, but he showed no emotion except hatred. Fernley could not endure the sight of his bared teeth, and was seized with a fit of vomiting as he waited for Quibar to speak. The guides questioned the wounded man in vain. He returned no answer, though it was clear that he understood. One of the blows on his head must have caused a partial paralysis, for he never spoke again, nor did he ever recover the use of his legs. Thus Fernley's secret was never told. On the contrary, as he muttered to me with his face in his hands, he was treated as a hero because of his endurance and gallantry with the rescue party. It is hard to imagine how he bore it, but he spoke as if his only sensation at the time was one of relief. What he could not bear was the malignancy on Quibar's eyeless face.

Those in charge of the wounded man said his constitution would not let him die, but Fernley had a conviction that he lived on the force of his will to hate.

Fernley's return to headquarters at Caracas, and thence to the States, was hurried and too like flight. But he was commended on his arrival for his ability to despatch. It seemed as though the world was in league to gloss his actions. He made arrangements through a firm of solicitors in Venezuela to pay a life annuity to Quibar sufficient to keep him and to secure him all attentions in his crippled condition. They wrote him a fulsome letter about his generosity, and his adventure and escape from death after the accident were topics that followed him and cropped up at every function, dinner, or ball that he had to attend.

This was in 1914, at the outbreak of War, and Fernley, impelled, like the Wandering Jew, came over and joined the British Army. Here as everywhere, he did well. He was *persona grata* at Headquarters, he seemed to do as he wished, and was out in France very quickly. He distinguished himself by the outrageousness of his personal courage. It was almost boastful, and he spoke of it to me with shame, for he had seemed to bear a charmed life, while he led others to slaughter. No one stood suspense or privation in the trenches better than he; for compared with what he had endured on that ledge of the Sierra Nevada nothing seemed long. He volunteered for all dangerous work, was a sharp scout and a hot fighter. He was idolised by the men, but devoid of any real human feeling. It was not till much later in his story that I found any trace of confidence or affection in anything he said.

He was mentioned in despatches, and was recommended for the Victoria Cross The occasion on which he earned it was when he had volunteered to lead a small party in an attack against a difficult machine-gun post that for weeks had been causing havoc. He seems, even at the time, to have felt this desperate venture as the touchstone of his fate, and in the thick of it, was calling on his few remaining men with wild unconscious shouts as he hurled his grenade at the gunner. The man nearest him echoed his shout. "Quibar!" was bawled by each as they hurled their grenades and followed up. The Captain stood for a second as if turned to stone, received a bullet in the side and went down. But the position was won, and he found himself the only survivor.

He received congratulations in hospital with an iciness that was attributed to modesty, and managed on his recovery to get himself transferred to another regiment. Any officer so tactless as to refer to his V. C. earned his implacable dislike.

The War ended, he spent like many others a period in London, living wildly and carelessly, received and fêted everywhere. The bravado of his manner was always atoned for by his good looks. He showed off and courted popularity, but was nauseated by his success.

Eventually he went out big-game hunting with a cinema firm. It satisfied his Wandering Jew's heart and gave him at the same time the publicity he craved without any personal contact.

One of his film engagements took him up the Orinoco, and a terrible compulsion seized him to go and look again; to see if the memory that had poisoned his heart were not fading out, whether so much expiation was enough yet. The re-entry into Quibar's room must have been the hardest ordeal of his life, and I presume that he found there, as he had known too well, an unchanging Nemesis. Where he went and what he did after that he never told me, and I had the mercy not to ask.

He took up his story from a much later period. He was in Leicestershire breeding steeple-chasers, still popular and successful, though I should say that the bitter lines I knew so well must already have been round his mouth. He made money, his picture was in all the daily papers, his colours were seen at every steeple-chase, and he rode his most difficult horses himself.

During this time a new element entered into his life. The urge to exact admiration from others, which he despised as soon as granted, had been one of the undesirable traits in his character, but he now, for the first time, found himself involved in the tenderest affection and homage. The force of this current amazed him. He was now forty years of age, and felt that his life was being entirely reintegrated. He had been, in adventure as in society, his own unhappy showman for fifteen years, and he longed for release. The girl to whom he brought his devotion was neither a beauty, nor a celebrity. She combined gentleness with rigid principle, in a way that is almost peculiar to women, and it was years after he first became attached to her before he allowed himself to confess his feeling.

Possibly he might never have done so, but one day he received what he could only consider as a reprieve—a letter from his solicitors in Venezuela to say that his unremitting accuser, after so many years, was dead. So overwhelming was his relief at the news, that all his self-isolation, his suspicion and his fatalism melted under its influence, and his tender avowal was made and reciprocated before he had fully taken in the significance. He was happy with the intensity known only to those who carry within themselves a dark background. But he was a prey to a new and dreadful nervousness. He became unable to sleep. His mind cried out in the night, that not so easily could he escape it.

There was a long halt when Captain Fernley reached this stage in his history. I had the impression that he was summing me up again, though he could not see me, and I tried to bridge this gap in our communication as well as I could by speaking, and moving, passing him the matches, and puffing at my own pipe. Eventually he collected himself, and went on as if every queer factor in his tale was another hurdle in a race. He was going through to the end.

"I went to stay with her people who had a country house outside Southampton. It was before Christmas and they had a large party of youngsters. It is extraordinary how little domestic life I have ever known. It was all quite new to me, and totally unlike the false simulacra of parties that take place in hotels, clubs and studios. With the exception of myself, everyone there had a genuine affectionate relationship with everyone else, and they all welcomed me with an openness that was almost painful to me. Honestly, that black apprehension came over me again. *She* made it all seem quite easy and natural and I put my heart into the thing, and made quite a hit with the kids. They played Blind Man's Buff, and I was blindfolded, and trying to put some go into it. The children were on their mettle and not to be caught. By-and-by I had an uneasy feeling that it was I who was all the time just escaping someone, not they. There was a strange scared silence in the room and I lost all sense of direction. I pulled up suddenly as if at the brink of a cliff, lost my balance, and putting out my hand was horrified to feel it was clutching a rope. It gave way, and amid an infernal clanging of bells in my ears, I fell and crashed my face against something hard and spiky. There was a general commotion; I had pulled the bell-rope out of the wall, and broken my teeth against the fender. My mouth was bleeding, and what I had said and what I looked like, I don't know, but I was shaking and she was looking at me as if she'd never seen me before. That is another look that I shall never forget. We quarrelled that night, God knows what about. I believe I swore at her. My toothache was raging. I took up the telephone receiver in the middle of the night and to the yawning operator said, 'In the Devil's name, put me on to a dentist.' The operator said I'd be lucky if I got anyone, they'd all be away for Christmas. Then after a pause, 'Yes, that's all right,' and she gave me a street and number and rang off.

"I went down half-dressed and got out my car, and drove into Southampton. I found a rotten old taxi and told the man to lead the way to this place and I followed. The streets were dark, there was no one about, and it was a quarter of the town I had never been in. He found the street and number, a sinister-looking place. There was no door-plate, but I rang the bell, and the door opened automatically like they do on the Continent. I stumbled upstairs towards a light on the floor above. The whole thing had become unreal as if I were delirious, what with the dark, the silence, the pain redoubled by the cold air, and the monstrous feelings I had towards my fiancée.

"I went into the room where a tall man in careless dress, as if roused from bed, was standing with his back to me bending over some instruments. I remember I looked at him vacantly and without premonition, taking him for one of these hard men who do the job and waste no time. I sat down in his chair with my head in my hands. Presently he chose his instrument and, reaching out one hand for his shaded light, he turned it full in my face and advanced behind it. I put my head back for him, and felt his hands move with a horrible familiarity over my face. Only then I looked at him, and for one moment saw again that eyeless mask with its bared teeth, before his fiend's fingers found what they wanted."

Captain Fernley pushed the black shade off his face and for the first time I saw the character of his mutilation.

"I never went back to her," he concluded, taking away the hand with which he had covered his scarred and hollow sockets, and accepting the whiskey that I held out to him. "I gave the police all sorts of false information. What else could I do? It was a queer thing," he added, as though it were quite an irrelevant detail, "they found my car at the top of a cliff, and me at the bottom. And now you can certify me if you like. It won't make any difference."

Many Coloured Glass

The Mayor's ball was to be held in the Costume wing of the Museum. This was occasionally used for concerts of chamber music, and as the Mayor was also a director, it had been found possible to allow its use for a private dance to celebrate an unusual occasion. The Mayor's only son was not merely coming of age, but had recently returned with an Olympic medal. A crowd of local enthusiasts had surrounded the station for his arrival, and newspaper photographs of his smiling response to the town's welcome were pinned up in every girl's office or bedroom.

Only a minority could hope for an invitation to the ball. The Mayor, Sir Joshua Waters, was fanatical about having public functions well done. He dreamed of being remembered as a mayor who had style. His invitations, therefore, were sent chiefly to those who could afford a real costume, or if their name made an invitation essential he would tactfully suggest the use of costumes "not included in the showcases", which in fact he had himself bought for the occasion. He let it leak out that he hoped guests would pay proper attention to the period of their dress. Everyone was to come as a character out of Jane Austen's books. He had bad dreams about important people in scruffy rag-bag get-up. Important people should look important.

Jane Austen's period had been chosen because the largest of the Costume Museum's many rooms was given to the period 1750-1830, also because in the attics of family mansions round about some relics—wedding dresses, uniforms or riding coats—might still be found. Sir Joshua was to appear stern but benign as Sir Thomas Bertram of Mansfield Park, his son Philip as Mr. Darcy, both specially tailored. As he looked at his son with pride, he congratulated himself that a desirable engagement would almost certainly be settled on the night. He had given his son a hint that the opportunity should be used.

As the hour approached Sir Joshua took a tour round the Museum to see that everything was in order. The main room faced the terrace and beyond that, the road. The tall Georgian windows were uncurtained, so that the people outside could watch the show. All round the walls were glass-fronted cases, each containing a period scene—a morning call, a christening, a family dinner, a stolen rendezvous, the sailor's farewell. Each scene had the furniture proper to it, with looking-glasses on the wall to show the other side of the costumes. There all the dummies sat or stood, in their best clothes and with their best manners, fixed forever as if waiting for the last trump. Normally they were lit by concealed electricity, but for this occasion candlesticks and candelabra had been put in the cases, adding more animation than one would expect, and chandeliers hung at intervals down the main room. The custodian was going round lighting everything up. The buffet was in the next room and the previous century, and there the inappropriate dummies had been hidden by scenes. Sir Joshua tasted the food and wine and gave his last instructions, which included a strict warning to the doorman to admit no one without an invitation card. He took a last look of surprised pleasure at his own face graced by a discreet period wig, and prepared to receive his guests.

Crowds of the uninvited began to gather outside before the first guests arrived. Usually the majority of such onlookers were staid housewives come to have a free look and good matter for gossip, but this time, because of the fame of Philip Waters, there were packed ranks of youths and girls. The police had difficulty in keeping a way open for the arriving cars.

Sir Joshua could be satisfied with his guests. Their arrival was a real pageant. The less-young ladies in the excitement of their vast bonnets and ostrich plumes, their pelisses, empire busts and trailing skirts, by behaving according to their natures while forced to a different stance and movement by the altered balance of their rig, and chattering the more from this slight physical frustration, showed how truly Jane Austen had observed the species. The local Repertory Theatre had contributed a contingent of curled and dandified soldiers, sailors and clerics with young ladies on their arms. The local beauty was cheered when, as Emma, she was handed out by Mr. Knightley.

Meanwhile, Ann, the as-yet-not-quite official girl-friend of the hero of the evening, was sitting in her taxi as it inched along towards the entrance. She had not seen Philip since his victorious return, and was surprised by the disturbance in her feeling—a pounding excitement which was not wholly delight. A sudden volley from part of the crowd of WE WANT PHILIP was taken up and grew to an enveloping roar, which filled her with near terror. She hated publicity, and caught herself thinking that however wonderful it was that Philip was such a star, she almost wished he had been unsuccessful and that they were going somewhere together quietly as before. The stamping chant of the young men was broken by the thin screams of girls, and Ann realised that Philip must have come to the top of the steps to wait for her. At this her panic redoubled, and also her excitement, suddenly indivisible from the hypnosis of the mob.

From somewhere near came counter shouts: "Down with heroes! Down with snobs!" The Commissionaire opened her door, letting her out at close quarters in front of a crush of typical students, dishevelled, unwashed, buttonless, bold-eyed or shifty, defying every human tradition. After all, savages, she thought, are as clean as cats. She half rose to begin the tricky business of stepping out of a taxi with shawl, fan and reticule, the invitation card and the fare ready in her hand. With one foot projecting, her glance lit on a slight, very young man who seemed the animating centre of the student group. His face was surrounded by long frizzy chestnut hair such as Leonardo's angels have—though less celestially ordered; this was a wild halo, and his expression was to match, being of such seraphic freedom and gaiety that at sight of it everything else went out of her mind. There was a second's pause— long enough for the gaiety to evaporate and for eyes suddenly grave with joy to look into hers, which must have met them with the same expression.

The surprise was so great that she tripped on her long skirt, and was saved from falling by a delicate but grubby hand. Then the gaiety came back, but Philip was there, proprietary.

No wonder the girls had shrieked as for a matador. Philip was really a figure to stun. Starting from the top, his hair had been drilled by the barber to fall in casual manly sweeps. It was fair and it shone. His face was held rigidly high by his built-up coat-collar and his stock, so that it was presented like something by Phidias on a stand. His shoulders were not too wide for grace, his chest and ribs so well adapted for holding and controlling breath that it was fascinating to watch the easy inflation and deflation under a coat that fitted like a second skin. The coat was cut away in front, as was then the fashion, well above the waistline and so exposed his hips and the whole line of his faultless Olympic legs in close-fitting cream jersey cloth.

If Mr. Darcy was thought arrogant because of his long tradition of eminence and responsibility, Philip Waters was arrogant unconsciously by virtue of his superlative physique and the qualities needed for successful competition. These, after all, he knew to be admirable things.

As he stood now at the top of the steps waving his acknowledgement to the crowd, he felt it was good to be able to offer a girl a part in his glory, even if only a walking-on part. He ran down the steps to meet Ann, and falling into the staginess of the occasion, bowed to kiss her hand.

"Go on, give her a proper one!" they yelled.

"All in good time," he called back good-humouredly, and led her up on his arm, very well pleased with their entry. He would have been less pleased if he had known that she had hardly been aware of their progress from the taxi to the big swinging doors. She could find no place, in the course and expectation of her life till now, for the experience of that timeless mutual look, too accidental to be given a meaning, yet it vibrated among her thoughts like a spring wind in an unawakened wood. How was she to orientate her actions now?

Inside it was a brilliant scene. The idea of acting up to the period was taking hold of the guests. They bowed and curtsied to the Mayor and also to each other as they gathered in groups along the side of the room, where the impression of number was doubled by the dummies entertaining each other behind the glass of their cases, and indeed seeming to entertain the Mayor's guests too, since these were reflected in the looking-glasses in their sets and must therefore be supposed to be present with them. The sailor's farewell, for instance, gained poignancy from a group of his mates waiting for him outside the display case.

Philip took Ann round with him on his arm as he went to do his duty to his father's guests and to receive from them the congratulations due to him.

"Aren't you lucky!" said the girls to Ann, rolling up their eyes. "Isn't he absolute heaven! You needn't blush, Ann, you're not the only person who thinks so."

The ball was to be opened by the old dance, Sir Roger de Coverly, followed by a waltz, which, though never stated to have been danced by Jane Austen's characters, was, nevertheless, growing in popularity during her lifetime.

For Sir Roger, two long lines were formed up the centre of the room. Philip led Ann to her position at the end and the innocent stylised flirtation began—the long solo journey down the centre to circle round one's opposite number without touching, with nothing but breathless smiles and the play of eyes, approaching and retreating several times, to achieve in the end a hand-in-hand gallop down the whole length and a parting bow. Such childish fun! Any booby could learn the steps, but Philip's hand was cool and hard, his look correctly genial, almost royal, and he moved with economy where other men romped or charged. Ann was glad of the formality of the dance, for she still had no idea what she might, in the course of the evening, let herself in for.

When later she and Philip were waltzing, her indecisions were far more acute, for he waltzed of course, as he well knew, divinely, travelling faster than any of the weaving and circling couples. Ann was swirled through the no-space of the crowd, guided by those inimitable shoulders and hips, feeling the pressure of his long light legs. She began to be intoxicated by the masterly movement and her own perfect submission to it. The dancers that passed across the mirrors in the cased sets imparted now a sense of movement to the lay figures, since they also had reflections which shifted to the dancers' eyes as they turned. If the figures themselves did not move, at least they seemed deep in thought, dreaming or remembering. In the overmantel behind the bent head of a girl reading a letter, Ann saw for a moment Philip's face bent over her own with an expression of deep satisfaction. With her, or with himself? And what was that girl remembering? But questions were left behind as they moved and swung together, while in the plate-glass front of the imitation world a swirl of much thinner, broken, half-recognised dreams flickered as they passed.

Every perfect waltz should end with a kiss. It is written into the last note. Philip drew her into the recess of one of the big windows. Because of the dark beyond it, the window seemed to those inside more like a huge pier-glass in which they saw only their bright selves like transfers on the surface, behind which a few wandering and irrelevant lights were passing through space. Philip's back was against the glass as he drew Ann's waist close to his, but she became aware that there was an outside world and tried to penetrate beyond the festive bubble in which she was enclosed, to the shadowy colourless movements out there, where the dark bulk of the trees only made the reflected chandeliers hang more brilliantly as if on the boughs. As Philip's hold tightened, suddenly she found and interpreted that crowded limbo, and what might have been the misty blur round a dim light was the Leonardo hair round a white face at a few yards' distance, watching what to him was ultra clear.

"What are you looking at?" said Philip. "Attend me!"

"It's too public here. All your admirers are still out there."

"Good luck to them."

"No, Philip, not now. Not here. *Oh dear*, that was a lovely waltz."

"Why *Oh dear*, in that tone? Why not 'You dear!', or 'my dear', my dear?"

"I don't know what I'm saying or doing," she answered.

"Then you want a few more drinks and you'll be saying what you really mean and won't know you've done it. I shall like that. But I shall have to leave you once or twice to dance with Father's old ladies. My father's position depends largely on the proper observances. My manager's a bit of a bully about public relations too. But I can't leave, you know—let's dance this."

This time it was a popular tune of the moment, and very strange and improper indeed did the dancing look in these most mannered costumes, as if Dionysus had got into the Assembly Rooms at Bath. The high bonnets with ostrich plumes and flying ribbons tossed and jigged, the bundles of curls flew up and down, the bosoms in front and sashes behind, the coat-tails and fobs and seals all jigged and swung, fichus slipped awry, trailing skirts were trodden on and ultimately had to be held knee high in mittened hands. Sir Thomas Bertram would not have approved at all, and indeed Sir Joshua shook his head, though this was not a giddy teenage dance and the stateliness of the Museum had a sobering effect.

"I must go now," said Philip. "Forgive me. There's my manager—I'll bring him to look after you till I come back. You needn't be jealous. I'm going to be horribly bored. Wait here by the door so that we can find you."

Ann leant thankfully in the comparative coolness of the doorway, which gave on to the entrance lobby. In spite of the drumming from the ballroom her ear caught the aggressive distaste in the doorman's voice saying, "Can I see your invitation card?" No "sir" she noticed.

The reply came with airy irreverent authority.

"Afraid I haven't one with me."

"I can't admit anyone without it. And fancy dress was specified."

"What do you suppose this is? Every banquet presupposes a beggar."

The accent undermined the doorman's confidence. You never could tell.

"Well, sir, shall I bring Sir Joshua to speak to you?"

"Don't bother."

Ann had come into the lobby, sure of whom she would see. She now came forward trading—with a pang of shame—on her being known as Philip's partner.

The boy bounded in and took her hand.

"Aren't we in luck," he said as he led her in.

In a moment they were dancing to the latest, wildest, most rhythmic hit, and from the start it was an inspired partnership. Their eyes never left each other, but their responding movements were as free as thought, as unexpected and as playful. They were two separate and equal people sharing an immense exhilarating Now-ness. This was laughter, this was delight, this was—most surprisingly—a flowering tenderness, and the rhythm was simply their lively young blood racing on its circuit.

If the other dancers noticed the infiltration of something not on the programme, it was only as an increase in their own acceptance of pleasure, but Sir Joshua had seen instantly that the style of his dance was ruined. He had devastated the doorman, who pleaded that Mr. Philip's young lady had overruled him.

"Torn jeans, no shirt under his sweater, beach shoes—no socks—it's an outrage! Spoils the whole show!"

"His rags are clean," the Mayor's partner replied soothingly. "Admittedly only from being washed by him in his own hand-basin. And he has an eerie charm."

"Where's Philip's manager? He ought to be able to deal with this. The press photographer is here, and you can be sure they'll make more out of Ann dancing with that layabout than of Philip. Ah, there he is—excuse me."

Meanwhile the dance had ended. In the recess where Ann had evaded Philip's kiss she received the lips of the stranger, and knew that he was now the magnet of her life, no other consideration whatsoever had either weight or pull.

"I shan't be able to stay here," he said. "Meet me in the garden behind the Museum as soon as you can. Here comes the irate Sir Joshua with a bodyguard—I must make my obeisance to him, and leave with dignity."

Ann laughed with delight at this picture, but Philip was disentangling himself from the beautiful Emma on the other side of the room. A waltz was beginning, and from Philip's face it was going to be a furious one. Oh, *no*, thought Ann, as for the first time her predicament fully dawned on her. She began to slip away through the crowd, looking in her white-and-silver dress like a darting fish, and the other guests with unexpected sympathy moved to let her pass.

She fled through the empty rooms of the Museum opening one out of the other. She did not know where the door into the garden was, but if locked that would be on the inside. How long, she wondered, would it take her Romeo to go round and climb the garden wall, or however he meant to get in after he had been turned out?

The sound of the waltz grew fainter behind her. In a corridor that she judged must lead to the back she stopped to collect her thoughts. Her heart was choking her. She sat down on a bench and hid her hot face in her hands, in confusion but not in doubt.

When she opened her eyes they were confronted by a musical box against the opposite wall—one of those early Bavarian toys where mechanical figures perform to the tune.

"How odd," she thought. The little stage showed a group of fiddlers, two couples in costumes like those of the ball she had just quitted, and in a doorway at the side, a gypsy beggarman.

Very faintly the distant waltz came to her ears, but no footsteps ringing in the abandoned halls.

With her hand pressed to her unsteady heart, acting under a sudden compulsion, she pushed down the lever. Delicate plucked music started up; the fiddlers sawed with their clumsy arms in time to an ethereal waltz. The couples moved jerkily out and each raised an arm to clasp its partner. To various clicks and rumbles from under the floor they began to revolve with each other and to orbit round the room. Their movements were sinister because of being both reluctant and predestined. Here they were and this was what they must do. Almost at once however, there was a whirring sound, a hesitation while the tiny figures stood quivering, then with a click and a jerk their motion was resumed. A moment later it was clear that something was going wrong. The fiddlers fiddled and the tinny music continued but there were sounds of misengagement, of metals in opposition, so that Ann was afraid she ought never to have set it in motion; the machine was out of order and might churn itself up. One of the couples divided—the lady flung off on an orbit of her own while her partner revolved on the spot, holding out his arms. To continued protest from the machinery the driven doll circled near the door. The beggarman had till now stood motionless except for an arm that jerked up and down, hat in hand, but now he was propelled forward, and after they had each twirled with arms outstretched, they met face to face and proceeded as partners. The whirring quickened as they sped round, while the abandoned partner revolved helplessly in the centre, wrenching against his imprisoning connection. He swayed this way and that as they passed him in apparently smooth working order. They passed the second couple, now ominously stationary. The beggarman seemed to have charmed his weird little stage, until they came again to the faulty point where she had first broken away. Inevitably she did so again, leaving him in the grip of the cogs near his enemy. These two then revolved round each other till they were face to face, when the box gave a screech and the legitimate partner fell upon the beggarman. The music stopped, and the last sounds were repeated metallic thuds as the beggarman's head was knocked against the floor.

And now Ann saw her own spectral face filling up the glass front of the box like a transparent stage-curtain. It wavered. She leant against the wall, appalled.

When she again began to consider where she was and what she was doing, she heard a confused murmur from the ballroom. It was like the sound in a sea-shell, not a party noise at all, and no music. From far away, but growing nearer and nearer and nearer, as in a nightmare, came the horrible tocsin of an ambulance. At the peak of sound it stopped, and there followed an interval of a silence more suggestive and heart-stopping than even the terror of its approach, before it set off again with its burden.

Ann leapt to her feet and began to run as if she could run after it. Then the band in the ballroom struck up with compelling desperation, as obviously taking action to avoid calamity as the ambulance itself.

The Italian Desk

S itting in the armchair in his bedroom, Francis Caxton studied the front page of the *Times*.

Cumberland. To be let furnished—immediately, with staff, for a few months—small country house. Two reception, three bedrooms, bath, main water, electric light. Garden, meadows, fishing. Moderate rent to careful tenants.

He was in London recovering from appendicitis and had been advised to take a long holiday in the country. This meant handing over his job to someone else, but he was just completing the term of his appointment on the staff of a mental hospital, and he was glad of an opportunity to write down the results of some of his observations; for he was a brilliant young man with a future. For the last few days he had been playing with all the possibilities put forward in the newspaper column. Many advertisers, he found, had quite a genius for warning him in advance as to the irritations or disadvantages of their offers of accommodation, by the very phraseology in which they chose to praise them.

Thus "an unrivalled position: 1 min. golf course" or "in house of gentlewoman near churches (two C. of E., one R. C.)" or "public schoolboy required by retired General and wife to share" were easily crossed off.

Francis Caxton had some private means, and he had also decided ideas about his own comfort. Perhaps he was selfish, for it consisted chiefly in being left alone. He liked playing the piano, he liked fishing, and he meant to read.

So he wrote to the advertiser in Cumberland. This gentleman's reply was attractive, the district was one that Caxton knew and liked, and there was a grand piano. He went up intending to look at the place, and to stay if it pleased him.

It was a simple grey stone house set in a sloping garden, mostly lawn. A big apple tree grew in front of the windows and two cedars a little lower down. The ancient stream crossed the road under a bridge just outside the gate, and filled the air with its babbling.

He was interviewed by a Miss Lacey, the house-keeper, a lady with a face like a plum both in colour and shape, he thought. Her hair was rather too emphatically not grey; and round her neck she wore a piece of velvet ribbon. Apart from being ridiculously refined she seemed a good sort of family retainer, loyal and particular. The house he liked. It was countrified, faded and gentle, and contained a medley of furniture and pictures from all over Europe. The pictures were a great relief. The larger part were good oil copies of Renaissance and seventeenth century work, and Caxton knew his London galleries well enough to tell that many of these must have been copied abroad. And yet the tone in which Miss Lacey referred to her employ-ers as "away" seemed to suggest that it was both unu-sual and not quite nice. Caxton liked them as he glanced round. He liked the odd things they owned and the way they had put them together; and he decided to take the house. When he had said so Miss Lacey relaxed her af-fected best manner for one equally affected but more familiar. She showed him "Miss Stephanie's" portrait, as though he were already, in a manner of speaking, one of the family. It was an oil painting in the dining room of a very charming girl with short curls and a gay and natural expression. He asked if it were recent, and she said, no, that it was done before. He discovered in time that when Miss Lacey said "before" in that final way, it generally seemed to mean, if he cross-examined her carefully, not within the last six months.

He chose from the three empty bedrooms the one that he preferred. It was light and square, with a large window overlooking the meadow and stream and a wide view of the fells. It contained a French carved wooden bed, long simple window-curtains, and lots of pictures. He gave his instructions and arranged to move in the next day. Miss Lacey was anxious to please him about the food. She delayed him a long time talking of it, and had for the subject a special voice, silky and far away. He deduced that he would be choicely fed, should his tastes happen to coincide with her own.

Caxton had brought a considerable variety of luggage with him in view of a long stay, and spent the next evening unpacking it in pleasant anticipation. He propped his fishing tackle in the side porch and opened the door for another long breath of the sweet moorland air; he stacked his music on the grand piano and tried its tone. Then there were all his books and papers. But Miss Lacey was at hand.

"The Master himself cleared everything out of the Italian desk, sir," she said, laying her hand on a large beautifully polished and ivory-inlaid table. "So you can use this," and she began to pull out the drawers, of which there were two rows on either side of the knee-hole, back and front alike. This gave him ample room.

"You can lock them all up," said Miss Lacey, "there's the key. It was Miss Stephanie's desk."

Caxton wondered vaguely why she always spoke as if Miss Stephanie was not expected back. He asked if she were married. "Oh, dear me, no," she answered, wagging her head and distending her eyes, "I'm glad to say."

They got the packing cases and mess straightened up, and the Doctor felt tired for he was still convalescent. He sat down to contemplate the room as it looked now that he was in possession. The double windows opened doorwise on to a terrace and were lightly shaded from a little distance by the boughs of the apple tree. He was a man very sensitive to his surroundings, and his eye wandered with satisfaction over the Bechstein, the Italian desk, the big French gilt mirror, the Chesterfield, and the bookshelves containing well-worn copies of the classic literature in four languages. Miss Lacey had ordered the fire to be lit, and it played on *famille rose* china and lent a soft animation to the pictures.

He had his supper opposite the portrait of Miss Stephanie whose intelligent and sensitive eyes seemed not to leave him. It was a delightful canvas, in which neither the artist's personality nor the sitter's was obtruded. You could look at it as easily as you might look at one person in a crowd. He felt quite grateful to it for looking back, and gave it flippantly a little bow as he left the table.

Afterwards he had a long smoke, sensibly doing nothing at all but lie on the Chesterfield with his feet up and listening to the purring of the fire beside him and the babbling of the brook outside the window, and seeing all the contents of the room through the rings of his own tobacco smoke he began to feel more intimate with his surroundings.

And yet when he went up to his bedroom on this early spring night, a feeling of sadness came over him. Let us suppose he was overtired, for he loitered in the middle of the room in a way most unlike his usual prompt resolution, undecided even where to hang his things. He sat on the bed for a long time deep in thought instead of getting undressed, and gazed round the four walls and ceiling as if seeking a tangible reason for his sudden melancholy. In this abstracted mood he was pulled up by realising that the small engraving he was staring at was an odd one to find in Miss Stephanie's room. It was number three in Hogarth's *Four Stages of Cruelty* engraved with great liveliness and relish. And now he saw that the set was complete, though unnoticed at first among the large oil paintings that covered the walls.

What a strange choice for a girl to put in her bedroom, thought Caxton; they were interesting enough in their way, but no one surely could like to look at those every night before going to sleep? They spoilt the charm of the room for him, and he unhooked them all and put them in a corner before he got into bed.

Next morning at his desk when Miss Lacey came in to see if breakfast had been to his liking, he told her he had taken down some of the pictures in his room and would be glad if she would put them safely away somewhere, as they were obviously of value as prints, though personally he did not like them.

"No, sir," she said, "nor do I; and I can't think how dear Miss Stephanie should choose them. She was such a sweet character, a real artist—all these oil paintings were done by her—such a sense of the Beautiful!"

Miss Lacey's versatile voice had a special register for the arts, and as Caxton looked from her rapt expression to the ribbon round her neck he understood that beauty was to her no everyday affair.

"So delicate, such a pure mind! I was quite horrified when she brought home those pictures. 'Aren't they quite fascinating', she said to me. Well! and those were not the worst."

She put her hand along behind the bookcase and drew out a large sheet framed in *passepartout* and arranged with a cardboard stand at the back like a calendar, which she handed to him. It was a series of little sketches by Leonardo da Vinci of all the stages of an execution by hanging, pitilessly realistic.

"She had it made for her desk," said Miss Lacey, with a quite ridiculous expression of secrecy and alarm. The Doctor hated cant and was moved to argue.

"It's the work of the world's greatest artist," he said. "He had to know both sides of life. A woman of education can surely frame any work of art she likes."

But he was not convinced by his own arguments. To look at, yes. To stand before you on your desk, no. It wasn't healthy.

"But there were worse than that," went on Miss Lacey; "there were things I couldn't possibly show you. Oh, real horrors! I can't imagine where she picked them up. Her father used to take them away in the end."

Having got so far, Miss Lacey's tongue ran away with her. "As a matter of fact, sir, since you're a Doctor yourself, there can be no harm in my telling you all, can there?"

And Caxton learnt to his stupefaction that Miss Stephanie had been taken to an asylum.

The young specialist did a good morning's work, but all the while as he wrote the notes on so many other cases, his mind was turning over the scanty information he had received about Miss Stephanie in connection with her portrait. The work he had undertaken actually was an attempt to classify the various forms of mental disease within certain well-defined physiological types, and Miss Stephanie seemed impossible to fit into any of these.

It was to be his system of work during his stay here to read one morning and write the next, and the afternoons spent in fishing or walking were the times when he digested what he had read or criticised what he had written. His evenings were spent in total relaxation at the piano, for which he had undoubtedly a great talent. As he sat before the keys, with candles burning on either side, it was the greatest delight to him to think that there were no flats above or below, and no neighbours, so that he could play as long as he liked with no possibility of disturbing or being disturbed. Miss Lacey indeed came in once or twice to sigh out how much poor Miss Stephanie would have loved to listen. "She was so artistic, but they say genius is akin to madness." She looked at the pianist as she spoke in sudden apprehension. But he assured her he was quite sane and asked her, if she thought it was not a presumption, to show him where Miss Stephanie kept her music. She did so, and he looked through it. Bach—Mozart—Chopin— "But she almost gave up playing at the end." He found several favourite pieces that he had not brought himself and took them out. As he was playing them through, there was a knock on the door, presumably the maid to clear away the coffee, and he called out "Come in" as he played on and took no further notice. But it happened several times, and at last he went to the door and found the little maid there. "Have you been knocking all this time?" he asked. "No, sir, I've only just come."

This furtive knocking happened several successive evenings, and was annoying though he took no notice of it. When it was the maid, she came in. Otherwise no one entered. But one evening as he was playing Stephanie's Chopin *Ballade No. 4* there was a knock on the window. He went in some irritation to see who was there, flung open the window, and seeing no one stepped out on to the terrace. He could have sworn he heard a throaty voice say "*Gratzia*" in his ear, but it must have been the branches of the apple tree creaking one above the other, for there was no sign of anyone. He went in again, puzzled and a little uncomfortable.

From that time onwards, almost as if he had let in an enemy, Dr. Caxton had an increasing feeling of being watched. He would constantly look up from his work in the morning as if someone were standing at the window, or in the evening from his music towards the big mirror opposite to make sure there was no one behind him. There seemed to be always sounds as of eavesdroppers, and at first he was inclined to suspect Miss Lacey, especially as he would often find the drawers of his work-table not quite closed as if someone had been at them. But really, the good woman was so obtuse, so content in expressing exactly the right attitude to everything, and so interested in the sensations of the dinner-table, that he couldn't imagine her spying; especially as there was nothing to watch. Also, as a matter of fact, he soon began to notice the same thing when he was out fishing. The babble of the stream seemed to conceal approaching steps, and every bush a leer. He felt impatient with himself, but the feeling remained.

One day, happening to drop the top of his fountain pen on the carpet, he got down on his knees to look for it, and thus found himself in a position where he could inspect the Italian desk more closely than he had thought of doing before. It was covered with a design of trailing sprays of flowers in ivory and mother-of-pearl, but he now saw that in the darker parts below the ledge of the table and below the bulges of the legs there were inserted into it Silenus-like faces, and these of such bestial imagination that he was astounded. There was a strong similarity between them, for they all had their tongues out, and a swollen strangled look. But some of them combined this with a horrible smile of pleasure. Francis Caxton could not remember ever to have seen so unpleasant a design carried out with such gusto. He now examined the desk intently all over, with professional interest, and found that much of the seemingly innocent pattern on the obvious surfaces of the desk was obscurely connected with the hidden theme, and once you had seen the key to it, it lost all semblance of decency. He came to the conclusion that it was unmistakeably the work of a homicidal lunatic, and his theory was that the laughing faces were portraits of the artist mimicking his victims. It was a better illustration to the worst type in his book than he could ever have hoped to obtain. And it astonished him that he could have worked at this desk for nearly two weeks without ever having noticed it. His thoughts went back to Stephanie. Had she ever seen these abominations? Was it possible she had bought the desk because of them? He went into the dining room to look again at her candid face, and admitted himself nonplussed. His mind was full of questions, and becoming aware that someone was behind him he turned to interrogate Miss Lacey. But the room was empty. "Damnation!" he ejaculated uneasily, unable to believe his eyes.

It was late April and he had formed a habit of sitting down for a pipe after lunch on the steps of the open French window with its pleasant view of the gnarled apple tree just coming into blossom. Miss Lacey brought in the coffee. "Tell me," he said at once, "where and when did Miss Stephanie get that desk?"

She seemed at least not to connect the desk with her rough-and-ready dates of before and after, for she pursed her face to think. "She found it" he learnt. "They bought the house ten years ago, keeping just a few things from the previous owners, such as the big three-fold mirror in Miss Stephanie's room that fitted so well, and fenders and stair-carpets and the like. And a long time afterwards, when they had lost touch with the previous owners altogether, Miss Stephanie found that desk in a disused attic under a lot of lumber. Fancy them overlooking such a handsome thing as that. And of course they could never pay for it, though they did advertise. Miss Stephanie had it cleaned up for herself. She used to be always complaining that somebody meddled with the drawers. As if I would allow such a thing! But I gave you the key, sir, because I understand professional work must be private." It was not often that Miss Lacey intruded long enough to be a nuisance, but now she stood as if there was something on her mind. At last she came out with it.

"You won't mind my saying so, sir, but it gives me such a turn when I come in to see you sitting there just like poor Miss Stephanie. That's where I found her, sir. I never saw anything so awful, her face was all swollen up and her tongue out"—(Caxton had leapt to his feet at this and was standing with his back pressed to the door-post)—"Yes, sir. The poor girl tried to strangle herself with her scarf. But we brought her round."

As Caxton took his rod and walked down to the stream he considered this gruesome revelation. To strangle one-self is a difficult undertaking. The arms are the wrong way on, and the grip would fail at the critical moment; as it apparently had done. But it was far easier to visualise a vic-tim caught unexpectedly from behind and half-strangled by someone else. The poor things in his asylum certainly tried every manner of violent death, including hanging, but not self-strangling.

His fishing was most unsuccessful that afternoon. The stream was exquisite, lambs were bleating and playing in the grey-green meadows, and primroses showed starrily among last year's tangle on the banks. But he could not command a moment's peace of mind. The loneliness and quiet indifference of the scene was only a foil to his misgivings; and when in reaching out to free his line which had become entangled in a willow, he put his foot through a loop of root and stumbled forward so that a pliant branch caught him around the throat, he uttered a yell of terror. Its echo followed from up the stream to deride him, but he was wet with perspiration and could not laugh.

He ate his dinner in misery. Stephanie's eyes seemed fixed on him in instant and significant warning. He saw himself joining her in the asylum if he could not pull his nerves together. He had no fancy for the piano that evening, all music seemed out of key and inapt. Also, though it is a strange statement to make about an eminent and authoritative young man, he definitely wished if he sat at all to sit with his back to the wall. He went up to his room to fetch his book which he had left there, and on switching on the light was attracted by something he thought he saw in the glass across the room. This was the three-fold mirror mentioned by Miss Lacey and the angles of reflection divided between them such an intricate cross-work of repetition *ad infinitum* that he had often been puzzled to find in it his left or right side.

It now seemed to him that in one of these distant mirrors of mirrors there was something reflected that was not in the others, and this was something he must urgently examine. He involuntarily moved closer—as if one could be nearer any point of a reflection—and his face came large and suddenly into view facing all ways in innumerable frames, and over the shoulder of one he saw the purple brow, protruding tongue and demoniac smile of the face on the desk. He spun round on his heel, beating the air with his arms, and bolted from the room, leaving the light still on, and without his book. When he had a little collected himself he rang for Miss Lacey, and told her, without allowing any of the palaver that was usual to her, that he was to have his bed made in one of the other rooms, and would sleep no more in his own. And, he added weakly, that while she was up there he would be obliged if she would bring him his book. She looked deeply shocked and grieved but made no demur. Caxton himself took a large stick and went out to the nearest telephone, where he rang up his friend Rooke in London asking him to come for pity's sake and spend at least the weekend with him; and this Rooke agreed to do and promised to travel that night, Friday, on the night train.

His new room was in every way less agreeable than the other. It was gloomy and lacked the grace of the rest of the house. But it had what in his present condition he found himself with amazement considering as an advantage. It had Miss Lacey on the other side of the wall.

He read till very late, making a great effort of will to concentrate entirely upon it. But at last his tired brain would serve him no longer. The dubious solitude and the mysterious midnight creaks took hold upon his imagination and drove him upstairs to bed.

He put out the light lest in giving way to his fears he should lose control of them. His mind was tossed between the instinct to discipline himself, to choose what he would believe and reject all feelings that he could not rationalise, and to treat himself as he would treat any hyper-neurotic;—or, on the other hand, to accept the strange, to face up in a scientific spirit even to those manifestations that science could not recognise; and spirit possession was one of these. He felt himself almost convinced, was determined, if possible, to investigate it; to confide in Rooke who would be there by mid-day tomorrow. He would get in touch with Stephanie's father and see her if possible.

In the dead of night his thoughts took on a terrible lucidity. That mind had power over matter he well knew. But was it possibly within the power of a fiendish spirit to strangle a living body? To admit that would be as fantastic as to admit that he could hear someone breathing in the room now, by the door. For some minutes past, that was just what he had been refusing to admit. He reminded himself sharply that he was considering Miss Stephanie's case, not his own. Besides, this was not the room that had the "associations".

The draught rustled in the casement curtains and drew them together so that the light rings slid along the rod and the folds fell back into place with a sound like a gentle sigh. That was odd, too. Against his will he heard his thought as clearly as if he had spoken, saying, "so, *she's* here too." Of course it was all morbid imagination, and it was absolutely essential that he should keep his head. But it did sound like suppressed breathing. Sometimes people hear their own breath against the sheets and think it is someone else. He held his breath, and refused to believe what he heard. An irrational paralysis prevented him from moving his hand to put on the light. He could only listen, and unreason wholly conquered him. The wheezy breath vividly expressed growing excitement as it approached. He stiffened in bed, gripping the sheets, and sweat broke out all over him as he felt two plump and furtive hands feeling up his chest towards his throat. Then indeed he yelled and fought like one possessed, but they had him and held him. And his assailant still had breath to chuckle as Caxton passed from an agony of insane revulsion into unconsciousness.

When Dr. Rooke arrived next day, all that he could do for his poor friend was to put him under control.

He himself was inclined to be suspicious of the part played in this tragedy by Miss Lacey, especially when he learnt that this was the second case within a few months. It was she who had been found in Caxton's room struggling with him, but of course she said she had been aroused by the noise. But even supposing that Miss Lacey had attempted murder, that would not account for Caxton's loss of reason. He obtained the information necessary to put him in touch with the doctor in charge of the previous case, hoping to have notes for comparison. The reply informed him of the patient's unexpected death. "She had been subject lately to periods of restlessness, followed by deep trance-like sleep. She was in this state on Friday night, and at about two o'clock in the morning the nurse in attendance was roused by a sigh. The patient put her hands to her throat, gave a long convulsive shudder as if in pain and terror, and so died."

The Tiger-Skin Rug

We really had gone to the view day before the sale at Vale Manor in the hopes of finding some honest chairs and well-made chests of drawers, but from that point of view it was disappointing; the furniture was poor, commonplace stuff. The only interesting feature of the house was the collection of stuffed animals. Big game hunting had been the owner's absorbing passion, for there were horns and antlers, heads and feet of almost every wild beast and several enormous glass cases containing tigers, lions and antelopes that had been mounted with incomparable skill. You stood your stick in an elephant's leg and hung your hat on a stand made out of four buffalo heads arranged back to back. It was a most imposing piece, and I said, to tease my wife, that I intended to bid for it.

The place looked more like a museum than a sale. Crowds stood gaping at the exhibits but obviously with no intention of buying; though there was a well-stocked wine cellar that might bring many to the actual sale.

In a small room containing a collection of native weapons, the walls bristling with spears, arrows, drums and shields, my wife's eye was taken by a rug of curious and wonderful workmanship. It was composed mainly of a large and very beautiful tiger skin spread fully out, and set into a background of patchwork fur almost as fine as a mosaic; a curving line of flat ivory pieces was cunningly set in to represent its teeth, and its eyes were ringed with white also and stared ferociously. Two skins cut into life-like silhouettes of monkeys with bright bead eyes were worked in on either side of its head and two young jackals flanked its zig-zag tail.

It was a unique thing, very soft and rich, and I could see at once by my wife's face that she was determined to have it. She is like a spoiled child when she goes shopping and, though I give in to her, I always pretend to the last moment to be obdurate, and she is always taken in. So we were playing out our usual farce when a parson, apparently a guest or next door neighbour for he had no hat on and was drawling along to his companion as one who had known everything intimately, turned his flow of reminiscence towards our rug.

"Ah, yes! dear me!" he said, "there is something that might interest you; the old Colonel used to be very proud of that; he said it was the finest tiger he ever saw, and he got it single-handed without even a beater or gun-boy. The natives would not have anything to do with it because one of their tribesmen had 'gone tiger' the week before and they felt superstitious about it. Gone tiger? Oh, yes! Oh, yes! quite common. When a native is turned out of the tribe for some misdeed, or goes mad, or something of that kind, he goes off into the jungle and they say comes back as a tiger to revenge himself. You should hear them beat their gongs when they think there's one about. Shocking! I came across a case when I was at the Mission in Cheieng Kong. The natives say they can tell when it is a tiger-man because the monkeys don't run away from it; they know it's out for man murder and they think themselves safe. That's why he had those monkeys' figures put by its jaws. Yes! rather a boastful idea, I quite agree, these big game hunters get like that. Poor old Colonel! when he was in his cups his boasting was dreadful. Ah me! we are all sinners! He took a dislike to that rug afterwards and had it locked in here. I remember him one night, when he had had too much, standing in here rocking from his heels to his toes saying, 'See, Padre, you can't have too many spears round a tiger.' A sad case. Well, he had his good points."

I had nudged my wife's elbow several times during this dramatic recital for the Parson was obviously enjoying himself. They held up a corner of the rug to examine the workmanship and the beautiful striped golden coat fell into soft moving folds.

I released my wife from her suspense, and we moved off to find someone who would bid for us. I spoke to a burly man in respectable plain clothes, who looked as though he might be a detective or auctioneer's foreman, but he was, he told us, the ex-butler, taking a last look round, and he obligingly offered to pass on to a decent dealer any instructions we cared to give. I gave him my card with "Lot No. 240, Chinese Tiger Skin with Monkeys" written on it. He read it and handed it back to me.

"Don't you have it, sir," he said. "It's a bad piece of work."

"What do you mean?" I asked, "it looks in very good condition."

"Well, it's had too many stories told about it, and where there's stories there's bother. We have lost good maids over that rug."

"It did the old Colonel no harm, did it?" said my wife. "Didn't he die a natural death?"

"Well, if you call it that," the butler replied. "A tiger finished him in the end. He couldn't keep away from them; he went back to Mandalay."

"Well, I am much obliged to you," I said, "all the same," and I gave him my card again and two half-crowns.

"As you like, sir," he said, moving off.

In due course a long yielding bundle was delivered to our little station.

"What's this?" said a porter jocosely, as he lugged it out of the van in jerks. "A body?"

It was lashed with ropes in the oddest way.

My wife and I later unpacked it together, pleased with the anticipation of trying it about the house. I must say I wondered when we first spread it out whether we had not made a mistake in purchasing it. It looked out of place in our very ordinary house, for I was neither a sportsman, nor had my wife any Chelsea notions of decoration. She is a comfortable, comfort-loving woman and all fur appealed to her, whether it was an opossum coat collar for herself or bedside sheepskin mats for the children's feet. This rug she intended for her own room which was large and rather badly lit for its size, the low square windows facing into the wood which surrounded the house at no great distance on three sides.

She set to work at once to adapt the room to her new purchase; the beds had to be pushed aside to make more floor space.

"Something will have to go, that's all," she said as she surveyed the new effect, but actually all that she ultimately removed was a reproduction of Botticelli's *Madonna and Child* which had previously always hung over our little girl's bed in its old position. We have one child of our own, aged four, whom we named Julia; and my first wife had died leaving me a stepson, Brian, who being deprived of both his natural parents had been adopted by us and took the place of the son of the house. He was now fifteen, a handsome boy, and we were very fond of him.

Our house was situated well away from any main road and at a little distance from the village, so our natural neighbours were foxes, pheasants, owls, woodpigeons and squirrels. Jays and badgers were not uncommon, for the coverts were high with bracken and little trodden, and the hollows dense with willow and willow-herb.

It was the beginning of a sudden July heatwave which grew daily hotter and I was thankful coming back from town in the evening for this cool and informal retreat, where the only urban intrusion was a motor-van from a local store, and an ice-cream cart that had weekly appointments with the scattered farm children and passed our gate every Wednesday ringing a hand-bell.

In this unfrequented spot imagine our surprise one evening when we heard the wheezing and strident notes of a popular air suddenly start up, and there came into sight along our drive, that figure of Victorian childhood, an organ-grinder with his monkey.

Julia ran out full tilt and then stood hesitant in front of him for a shy stare, while the man, who looked like a Malay, turned his machine more rapidly and shifted his wandering gaze up at the windows with that meaningless and idiotic grin so often seen on these hapless aliens.

My wife came out with a banana for the child to give to the monkey. Julia, upbraided by Brian for cowardice, presently advanced to within reach of the chain and held out the banana which the monkey seized, and then, with inverted gratitude, turned and bit her sharply in the finger. My wife darted forward with her hand upraised to strike it, but it took a bound on to the Malay's shoulder and off again; the collar round its waist broke and away it went with its tail in the air across the lawn and up the nearest tree.

Julia, thoroughly hurt in her feelings of right and wrong, was hurried indoors for an application of iodine, while Brian, myself and our gardener, Bibby, helped to coax and chase the monkey. It evaded all our devices and chattered malignantly at us from tree to tree as it worked its way deeper into the wood.

Eventually I had to order the Malay off the premises; we had dismissed him politely at first with a glass of beer and half a crown to console him, but he understood so little of what we said that in the end I had to resort to threatening attitudes most distasteful to me, but I now felt less confidence in his imbecile looks. He was probably a rascal and practised this trick in every country place, coming back at night with the excuse of the monkey and taking away with him whatever it and he could lay their hands on.

He went at last, and as he turned into the lane he shifted his organ on to his back, and intoning some native chant, he punctuated his shuffling steps with rhythmic leaps and stamping, and so passed out of sight. It occurred to me to go in and ring up the police to warn them of a possible pilferer, but perhaps he considered the loss of his monkey had ruined his trade, for he did not pass through the village and no one else in the district saw him.

The antics of this departing figure with a load of mischief on its back kept recurring as a subject of conversation during the evening. Brian gave a spirited imitation of it to Julia when she was being dried after her bath. My wife said, "Don't do that, Brian, you'll give the child nightmares," but she always said "Don't do that" to everything; it was the regular accompaniment to our laughter and quite ineffectual. I think often she hardly knew when she said it herself; but Julia was far from having nightmares; she played monkey sitting on Brian's shoulder and taking great leaps from there to the springy bed and exhausted herself with peals of laughter; then with a biscuit in each hand for her supper she dumped herself down on the new rug and, pleased with its softness, put her head down to turn somersaults; the yellow curls on her little head fell forward and lay softly mingling with the fur so near them in colour. If my wife had bought it especially to shew off Julia's childish beauty, she could not have done better.

Julia had paused in the first position of the somersault, her eye attracted by the tiger's ivory teeth over which she began to run her finger, but my wife snatched her hand away saying "Don't do that", at which we all laughed, and she blushed and said she supposed she was still thinking of the monkey.

We were all late that night, for there can be few things like a monkey hunt for wasting time. We were not ready for dinner before nine and it was nearly twelve when I said to my wife "Good Heavens! look at the time." I yawned and stretched myself and rose to see to the locking up, when the door bell clanged loudly. I went to open it expecting perhaps the night constable, but a tall stranger stood there, who, raising his hat and speaking in an unusually deep and vibrant tone, addressed me in a manner that left no doubt of his breeding. He apologised for disturbing me at that time of night, but might he use the telephone as his car had completely broken down. Our telephone was in the sitting room and so I led the way there. My wife looked at us enquiringly and smiled without waiting for my explanation in her habitual frank and friendly way.

The stranger was dressed with distinction, even elegance, and had something of military correctness in his bearing. He bowed to my wife with renewed apologies, and while I stood with the receiver at my ear I listened to his explanation and took stock of his appearance. It was both striking and vaguely familiar, and I felt it from the start to be as attractive as it was in some way repellent; and this was my wife's first impression too, as she told me later. His physique was magnificent and his profile might have come off an Etruscan vase so pure was the line from brow to nose; but his eyes had a cat-like upward tilt at the outer corners and his sleek hair was in even ripples of the darkest red, a violent colour, more animal than human. A white streak running backwards through it from the temple, a relic of some former wound or shock, made his head all the more arresting. Under his short red moustache his mouth had curves that were not reassuring, but when he smiled in reply to my wife's sympathy he drew the corners of his lips back over his teeth in a way that was peculiar and taking.

He was on his way to some friends about forty miles distant, had been held up by constant engine trouble and now could get no further. He wished to get a taxi to take him to the nearest hotel. But here his bad luck followed him for I could not get any answer from the exchange for all my ringing, and was wondering how much help one ought to offer to a total stranger of intriguing appearance, when it leaked out in conversation that the family he was on his way to visit were well known to us by name, friends of friends, and at once the whole position was altered. So strong is the social feeling among educated people in the counties that a familiar name acts like a password.

We felt now that it was too late for him to move on anywhere that night and my wife pressed him to let us put him up. I poured him out a whiskey, and as I considered the nuisance it would be to me if I had to get out my car and drive him to the nearest inn, I became as hospitable as she. He demurred very much at putting us to such inconvenience but in the end he acknowledged his gratitude, and when we had pushed his car into shelter and he had hung up his hat and coat in the lobby, we settled down again for another half hour in the new roles of hosts and guest. He was at once at his ease and his deep purring voice and alert politeness were pleasant to hear and see. There was a deprecating quality in his attention as if conscious he was not acceptable to all, and yet I felt he was a man who could rarely have been unsuccessful. I judged him to be of frank intention and I enjoyed his presence. I have described him perhaps at greater length than you have patience for, but I tried that night in vain to analyse the very strong impression he made on me.

As we rose to say goodnight my wife reminded him that we did not yet know his name. "Dr. Sathanos," he replied with a bold frank smile at her as if aware that the extraordinary name fitted him too well. "A very old name; my father was a Greek and my mother Scotch." He passed his hand apologetically over his hair with a wry look.

We gave him a bedroom on the ground floor, the only one at liberty in the holidays, and my wife warned him jokingly to close his windows if he was afraid of monkeys; but he replied that it only needed that to make him feel quite at home, he having only just returned from Rangoon.

But it was my wife who on opening her sleepy eyes in the morning saw the monkey squatting on her new rug, briskly turning itself about and clicking with satisfaction and interest. She started up and shooed angrily, but it did not seem frightened. It rose and walked deliberately towards the window, its arms hanging and its wicked little face grinning back at us, then slowly swinging itself up on to the sill it sat there a moment, gave a low squawk as if to say it would soon return, and sidled quietly out into the creepers.

I had little time for breakfast on weekdays, and when one is swallowing one's coffee too hot, now or never, manners are reduced to their minimum. But Dr. Sathanos with his strange and legendary face made breakfast an art, and rose so easily and so often to wait on us all, and had so many ways of considering everybody that I felt a boor beside him. He talked with charming equality to the children, and Brian was soon entirely under the spell both of his powerful physique and of his polish and experience. As for Julia she did nothing but stare at him, her eating and drinking was mechanical and unconscious. He passed behind her chair as he laid a plate on the sideboard and touched her sovereign-gold hair, remarking in his deep vibrant voice "That is the colour I love more than any other."

I said goodbye to him in a hurry and commended him to my wife's attention. When I returned that evening he was still there; his car could not be ready for a day or two and his friends, it seemed, had some domestic trouble and could no longer receive him, so my wife had asked him to stay till his car was ready, because he was company for me and so good to Brian. She was a great talker, never so happy as when there was something to say.

Young Dr. Wainwright had been in for a drink and a chat and had said there was an outbreak of tropical fever on the riverside and warned her to keep the children away from the cinema. He was worried because he hadn't much experience of it. He is a clever young man and always admits what he doesn't know, but wasn't it an extraordinary coincidence, quite providential, do you know Dr. Sathanos is a specialist in just that sort of thing and so kindly offered to give him any help he could. Dr. Wainwright was calling for him the next day. Of course one couldn't help thinking of that monkey; nobody knows what ship it came off or anything.

I asked her where everybody was now, for we were having tea in a quiet *tête-à-tête*, all the windows open wide because of the great heat and not a sound came through but the ring-doves cooing.

Why, she replied, Bibby had come to say there was a circus going past down by the priory gates and Dr. Sathanos had strolled down with the children. Should we go and meet them?

We walked along down a little bracken track, waving away flies that rose in hordes, and by-and-by we saw Brian swinging on a gate and Dr. Sathanos with Julia on his shoulder. Our neighbours, the Bensons, were there too with their enormous dog, a cross between an Alsatian and a Great Dane—a really majestic creature. Piebald ponies were trotting past, a camel and some tiny donkeys. As one of these tried to turn in at the gate Brian asked the man in charge where were the elephants.

"They've gone by the other way," he replied. "Funny thing, we had trouble with them a while back; something in the wind they didn't like and we had to humour them; never known it happen before."

At this moment the children were distracted from their disappointment by a menagerie van carrying jackals who, as it drew level, suddenly set up a commotion. They thrust themselves against the bars, and flinging back their heads the whole lot yelped. The procession had come to a momentary halt and their cage was facing Dr. Sathanos, towards whom all their outcry seemed directed. I can see him now standing in a smile which shewed all his teeth, and they were sharp and even.

"Why do they howl like that?" said Julia, who had turned rigid and slipped down off his shoulder to come to me.

"Perhaps they are home-sick," said Dr. Sathanos; "it's a long time since they followed a hunter," and he began to spin jungle tales to Brian's ever open ears.

It grew no cooler even by bedtime and as I lay awake disturbed by the high treble of the mosquitoes, I heard the wood outside as restless as I: there seemed a perpetual rustle without enough wind to make it; birds would start twittering from their sleep here and there; a nearby jay woke me as I was dozing, then a rabbit screamed—poor little devil, I always hate to hear them—and every leaf outside the window seemed to itch.

Another day as sultry followed. I hate heat myself but our guest came down almost purring with health, cool and obliging as ever. It is no use judging a man by his face or saying his mouth is coarse and bitter when every action he does denies it. He was certainly an original personality, a great character and a really good sort.

We returned from town together, he having been to the fever hospital, and tea was laid in the garden. As we were eating it Brian saw our friend the monkey peering at us from the trees; it ran along a spreading branch which hung over the lawn and great was our surprise to see it had found a companion. The two of them advanced by stages to Dr. Sathanos's chair where he sat with his back to them, but seeing us all pointing he looked back and tipped his chair until he could throw one of them a biscuit which it nimbly caught.

"Oh, don't do that," said my wife, "they might come again and give us all tropical fever."

"I beg your pardon," said the Doctor, "but if you don't like them we will soon get rid of them, as we learnt to do in the jungle."

He turned round and rested his hands on the back of the chair, leaning towards the monkeys like a great quadruped, and made a face at them in the horribly realistic manner of a snarling tiger. The monkeys went off in great bounds chattering their teeth at him and Brian laughed uproariously, but Julia, who had run round behind the Doctor's chair in order to get a better view, received this grimace at close quarters and was terrified almost into hysterics. The Doctor tried, with the rest of us, to pacify her, but about his smile perhaps there lingered still in her fancy a trace of fang and she screamed afresh at every advance.

Of course I know that when the heat passes a certain temperature in this country we all get snappy. My wife and I were vexed with Julia and annoyed with each other, but, in the long run, it was the monkeys who got most of the blame for this unfortunate incident. Where on earth could a second one have come from? It increased my wife's fear of tropical fever in as much as illogically she was convinced that an unknown source must be infected. So in the evening when Dr. Sathanos had retired to his quiet bedroom to write a report of Dr. Wainwright's cases, I went into the wood with an old army rifle, the only weapon I had, intending to shoot them.

It was an amazing evening for England, the sky was bright apricot and the level sun filled the wood with stripes and bars of shadow and glare. The midges rose and sank in columns and everything was amazingly silent. I really had quite a jungle feeling as I stalked this strange game, and was completing the circle of my stealthy round near our own gate when at last I saw the pair of them, their arms encircling a big bough and their cheeks laid sideways against it. The light was bad, but I was taking careful aim when a rustle in my wife's bamboo hedge behind me made them look in my direction and sidle to the safer side of the tree. I should have said that it was a large dog's tail I heard brushing backwards and forwards, but, if so, it was a very guilty dog, for, as I swore in my vexation, the sound withdrew from me. The bamboos quivered and stood upright again and nothing broke cover.

I knew I could never get those wily little devils now, so I turned in at the gate. Bibby was watering his geraniums by the side door.

"Does the Bensons' dog ever poach up there?" I asked.

He said, well, he couldn't exactly say he had ever seen it to be really sure, but he had seen something that was certainly very big and might have been him down in the willow covert the night before, when he came to look at his traps, but it is so full of willow weed, he said, you couldn't really say, not to be sure, when it was a question of neighbours. But I was vexed by losing my shot and answered that I should want him to take a note down to them in the morning.

That night was the first night on which we heard the howling. Everybody knows how a cat can make one's spine creep, but this was far worse and all the more eerie for being low and searching. It woke us both up; my wife sat bolt upright in bed.

"What's that?"

"It can only be a cat," I replied; "What else is there?"

She insisted that I should get up and look. I pulled up the blind; the moon, which was near the full, streamed in and fell on my wife's scared face, and cast a queer light on the tiger skin mottled by the shadows of the wisteria sprays which fringed the windows. I looked out and saw the lawn like satin, and the fir wood that struck its crests into the sky like so many jet black spears and stretched its shadow on the grass before it. Below the window each silver slab of crazy paving was clearly outlined and every little plant had its mat of shadow. All was still and empty.

I turned back to get into bed and as, in crossing the floor, I put my bare foot on the tiger skin I swore I stumbled forward. There must have been a mouse under it for it moved as if it were alive.

"I wish that damned cat was in here instead of outside," I said; "the place is alive with mice."

I was annoyed with my wife for making too much of a tale about that cat, for what else can it possibly have been? I could see Sathanos was laughing at her; his smile was too polite to be spontaneous, but, I felt, too bold to be quite polite.

After all she was his hostess; I flattered myself I was rather his sort, we had a great deal in common, but you have to know a man very well before you laugh at his wife. That grin of his shewing all his teeth was unnecessary, and it rather jarred; besides, though things looked different in the morning, I didn't like that howling myself, either that night or the next; in fact it was abominable, and the more I thought the less I liked it. I could only think of two causes; either it was a natural sound, made by an animal, in which case it was certainly one I did not care to have about, or else it was a supernatural one; it was diabolical enough, God knows, but a sane family man can't come down to breakfast and say that he thinks the devil's in the garden. I could see my wife had thoughts she didn't like to say and, of course, if she had said what I was thinking I should have answered with sarcasm, so she kept her thoughts to herself; but she was jumpy and said "Don't do that" oftener than usual, even when Julia ran across the lawn.

The next thing was that the cook left, refusing to give either reason or notice, and my wife was much upset at such a contretemps with a visitor in the house whom she so much wished to please. But as he had been most appreciative of her regime before, so he became the easiest to please now. Camp life suited him down to the ground, he said, and insisted on trying his hand as cook. Brian followed him, for the first time in his life seeing the kitchen as an adventure.

I wrote a rather strong note to the Bensons, asking them to keep their dog up, and took it upstairs to my wife to see if she thought they would be offended. It was a Saturday and she was counting the sheets with the housemaid.

"If you please, Ma'm," the girl was saying, "might we have Bibby in to put a piece of felt along the bottom of your door? There must be a draught blowing in, because your new rug won't lie flat. I can't keep it straight. It gave me such a start when I went in last night to see it heave up like."

"My good girl," I interrupted sharply, handing my wife the note, "it's as hot as an oven and there's no wind at all. Do talk sense."

"Well, sir," she finished lamely, "I didn't say wind, I said draught."

"I don't think I like it in here anyway," said my wife. "Not this hot weather—you don't want fur in your room. Take it down with you, Keith, if you're going, and put it over the couch in the sitting room."

I did so, and sent Bibby off to the Bensons with my note. The sun was torrid. For nearly a week it had been getting steadily hotter. After lunch even Sathanos seemed to feel it, though not uncomfortably.

He settled himself down on the fur-covered couch full length with his hands behind his head, the embodiment of strength and ease, and his deep magnetic voice was most soothing.

"Julia must go for her rest," said my wife—the invariable signal for disturbance—and Julia of course protested.

"Let her stay down and lie here," said Sathanos drowsily, rising from the couch and leaving an almost perfect mould of his head, shoulder and hips in the soft rug.

He bent down with a strange smile to pick her up and lay her in his place, but Julia turned mulish. She didn't want to lie down at all, she wouldn't be put on the couch; she tugged with sudden shyness at the wrist by which he held her. Meanwhile Brian, intolerant at the disturbance and annoyed to see his idol occupied with a baby, bounced on to the vacant couch and wrapping the rug round him, said provokingly, "Right. Then you can go upstairs. It will be all the better for us, we shan't have to talk baby-talk."

At this point something rather shocking occurred. Dr. Sathanos, as if giving way to an uncontrollable fit of irritation, crouched down and putting his face close to Julia's, directed at her his beastly murderous snarl. Perhaps it was only meant as an object lesson and a moral against naughtiness, or perhaps only as a bachelor's clumsy joke, but it looked like real malice and made a most unpleasant impression.

Her mother with a red face snatched her up as she fought for breath in choking terror, and hurried her out of the room.

"I'm sorry you did that," I said to the Doctor, who had walked to the mantelpiece and turned his back on us. Every man is touchy about his daughters, and I felt quite outraged.

"Camp jokes don't go down in the nursery, I'm afraid," he answered with a shrug; "I apologise."

He lit himself a cigarette and in the mirror I saw his pointed fingernails silhouetted against the window, and his slanting eyes fixed darkly on the unconscious reflection of Brian wrapped in the tiger skin.

I chiefly remember the rest of the day for the heat. There was no respite from it. The Doctor had atoned for his lapse of temper by doing more than his share of the work, and before long my wife was smiling her gratitude.

How could one not like him for his jovial adaptability? He was an amiable and proficient cook and butler, his footfall as silent as a native's. As the sultry day drew to a close, more and more his tall figure and enigmatical vitality dominated the house, and more and more a dread and presentiment closed in upon us with the night. Brian particularly seemed restless and wan, especially when the Doctor was absent. I remember we teased him for it.

In bed my wife talked and turned, wanted me to throw back the blankets, alter the blinds, open the door, anything but settle to sleep. I knew quite well what it was that kept her in suspense. I rather thought I heard a slight noise downstairs too, and I determined to keep watch; so lifting Julia into my wife's bed—an instinctive action, there was no sense in it—I slipped between the blind and the window, armed with my rifle.

The moon was at the full, riding among high clouds that travelled slowly on the hot wind; it blew in gusts through the window. Two owls called and answered across the garden, their ghostly too-whoo's tracing the direction of their flitting. All else was silent, and set as if for a crisis.

Frequent meteors fled across the sky, their journey never finished. The leaves rustled in my ears and a spider's thread trailed across my face. Suddenly a jay's harsh note rang out across the wood, tearing the silence with warning. We knew the signal, and I waited in agonising tension for what seemed an age; and still too soon that wild and howling cry swelled out from somewhere close below the window—enough to draw the very soul out of a man, and my heart stopped beating when I heard it. Again and again it came, from here and there, and presently I realised that a slight figure had come out on to the lawn and was standing alone, the moonlight falling full on his face and rumpled hair. It was Brian, walking slowly in a dazed way, and looking helplessly round as if someone had been calling him. I leant out to shout to him, but he seemed not to hear; he had started back a step and was staring as if fascinated into the bushes below me. Now he turned and began to run, looking backwards towards the house as the object of his terror drew its long body out of the shadows. Two or three relentless bounds across the lawn overtook him, and with an infernal cry it bore him down. I fired convulsively. Cry and shot re-echoed through the wood and the heaving mass was still.

My wife lay sobbing through her chattering teeth as I rushed out of the room, stumbling down the stairs in the dark till I stopped to put my hand out to feel for the electric switch at the bottom. Then I saw with a shock of new fear that I had almost run into a silent unexpected presence, for the moon shone through the fanlight in the hall, and fell on the red hair and pockmarked face of Dr. Sathanos bent close to mine, his lips drawn back nearly to his ears in a hateful smile at my undisguised fear.

"Sathanos!" I shouted as I switched on the light—but there was no one there.

"Sathanos! Sathanos!" What a name to echo down one's hall in the dead of night! But no one came. I turned on all the lights and ran from room to room, but his had a disused look, and all were empty. Outside I saw Bibby, roused no doubt by my shot, and hurrying out from his cottage. He was on the lawn before me. He looked strangely at me as I came up, and I saw that what lay at his feet was the tiger-skin rug, wet with dew, and under it we found the body of Brian, dead, with a bullet-wound through his head.

It was days after this tragedy before I spoke to my wife of Dr. Sathanos's disappearance, but she too looked queerly at me and seemed to shrink from me, as if I had said something unforgivable or opened one of those subjects whose existence can never be acknowledged.

The Horned Man

or

Whom will you send
to fetch her away?

A Play in Two Acts

DRAMATIS PERSONAE

SIR MARTIN WESTBURY
FRANCIS, his son aged eighteen
PHILIPPA, his daughter aged fifteen
BESS, his daughter aged thirteen
JENNY, his daughter aged ten
MR. SIMON UPJOHN, King's Agent
MISTRESS ALICE, governess and housekeeper
OLD MOTHER ALISON TAYLOR
WALTER, a page in Sir Martin's house
COOK
ROBERT BALL, a lout
GEORGE CARPENTER, a wizened boy
MAT PRICE, a snivelling boy
BEN GOOSE, a booby
TOMMY VINES, a small talkative hanger-on
JUSTICE GIRTH, a very fat man
JUSTICE FEVER, a neurotic
JUSTICE DE GROOT, a punisher
A PHYSICIAN
A KENNELMAN
A SECRETARY
WITCH SEARCHER, WITCH PRICKER,
CONSTABLE, MAYOR, PARSON, CROWDS

THE SET

The scene is the ante-room to the Tudor hall in Sir Martin's house.

Across the back runs the partition screen with a balustraded gallery from side to side, an exit at each end. Under the gallery is the central door to the hall, the back cloth showing hammer beams. Just left of this door is a staircase at right-angles to the gallery and opening into it. The bottom post of the stairs (left) serves to support the floor of the girls' bedroom, level with the balcony and opening on to it. The bedroom has a lattice left. Underneath the bedroom is the still-room with door front and exit back.

The ante-room has a main outside entrance up right, a lattice window down right and an exit to kitchens down left. The fireplace is imagined at the centre front.

Two Tudor chairs, a small table, a bench.

A light-coloured curtain across the door at the back will serve as a background to the magistrates' rostrum in the court scene, and also to show the minotaur's shadow in the last scene.

Jenny's room is supposed off gallery left.

As this is a close-knit family affair, the running up and down stairs and from one room into another is important.

If the suggested set is too elaborate for an amateur production, rostra can be used instead.

Note on the Masks

Alice's mask can be cut off at the point of the upper lip, following the lines of the cheek. The hair to be as long as possible.

Upjohn's mask to cover his shoulders. As the muzzle will rest on his chest, a white gauze blaze on the forehead will serve to see and speak through.

The ghost's mask to be waxen, with a toothless rictus and wild white hair.

The action takes place in the reign of James I.

Act I
Scene I. The ante-room in Sir Martin's house.
   II. The girls' bedroom.
   III. The ante-room, next morning.
   IV. The girls' bedroom.
   V. The ante-room, next morning.
   VI. The girls' bedroom.

Act II
Scene I. The Court Room in Sir Martin's house.
   II. The ante-room.
   III. The Court Room, two days later.
   IV. The ante-room.
   V. The ante-room, later.
   VI. The girls' bedroom.

ACT I

Scene I

The ante-room in Sir Martin's house.

Philippa and Bess looking listlessly out of the window. Jenny on the stairs nursing her dog.

Philippa

(*leaves the window to sit by table*)

I am sick of everything. This everlasting flat damp view! Nothing to look at. No one coming in. No one even going past. Nothing but mud outside. Nothing but sewing in. When will anything ever happen! Dominos!

(*Dog barking outside*)

Bess

Come back, Philippa. Come and look.

Philippa

What at?

Bess

What are those boys chasing? They are pelting some-thing, or somebody. Can you see? All huddled up.

Philippa

It's an old woman. Oh! What an old fright. Got her! Got her again, right in the mouth!

99

BESS

I wish I was a boy. They can do what they like. Open the window. What can I throw? An apple.

(*Philippa opens the lattice and Bess throws. Philippa imitates the old woman's defensive actions. Bess hops in excitement. She throws again.*)

PHILIPPA

She's as easy to hit as an old sheep. Oh! She's fallen backwards into the ditch. The boys are running away. Look out! It will be Father.

(*They close the lattice hastily and stand back giggling.*)

(*Enter Sir Martin right, Walter centre back.*)

PHILIPPA AND BESS

(*curtsying*)

Good evening, Father.

JENNY

Father! (*She runs towards him but is caught by Philippa and Bess.*)

PHILIPPA

You didn't curtsy. We have to, so must you. Again, properly.

(*Jenny runs and clasps her father.*)

SIR MARTIN

Good evening, my pet. Good evening, girls. Wait a moment, Sweetheart, till I get my wet things off.

WALTER

Your cloak is covered in mud, Sir. Have you had a fall? I hope you have not hurt yourself.

SIR MARTIN

No, thank you, Walter. But just outside here my horse shied and slipped, and I came off. It was so near my own door that I wasn't expecting surprises, but the horse was frightened by an old woman who had fallen in the ditch. I wondered what it was myself, flapping about there, legs in the air. Some boys were walking away looking too saint-ly-smiling to be true, so I guess they had been plaguing the poor old dame. Will you go and find her, Walter, and bring her in to the fire to dry herself and warm up. Tell Cook to give her something to eat.

WALTER

Yes, Sir. (*Exit left.*)

SIR MARTIN

Boys seem little better than a herd of wild dogs. They'll worry anything they can.

BESS

We saw them through the window. I knew that it was very wrong.

SIR MARTIN

I am glad girls have more piety.

JENNY

Father, when you were a little boy, were you cruel?

Sir Martin

I am afraid so, once or twice, to try. But I didn't like the feeling, so I stopped. My mother was like you, she couldn't bear it.

Jenny

Where have you been all day?

Sir Martin

At the Lord Lieutenant's, discussing very nasty business. I am weary and sick with it, and fear we may be in the middle of it here for a long time. I was glad to be coming home again to you.

Philippa

(*to Bess*)

We're to be in the thick of something anyway. That's better than nothing.

Jenny

What is it, Father? May we know?

Sir Martin

Ah, my dear, you can't fail to know, and I am afraid you will be as distressed as I am. There is to be an organised witch-hunt, to clear the Fens of witches.

Philippa and Bess

Witches! Ooooh!

Sir Martin

And that means that no helpless old woman will be safe. And even some handsome maids may be singled out, so don't think it has nothing to do with you, Philippa and

Bess. It's not justice, it's the Devil's sport.

JENNY

But, Father, are witches real? Can they really make people die? I thought they were only tales to frighten naughty children with.

SIR MARTIN

I believe in the Devil. And I suppose it is possible for people to be so wicked that they worship him, and receive from him unnatural powers. It is said that witches have a secret king whom they call The Grand Master, whom they reverence as the Devil's representative. As for their spells, their thorn twigs and finger-nail parings, their boiled blood and newts' eyes, that's all superstitious rubbish, however evil the intention. Though who knows how great the force of an evil intention may be, or where it stops?

The trouble with witch-hunts is that most people have only to be frightened for them to believe that what they fear is true. And if they don't exactly know what it is they fear, they can behave like madmen, and justice means nothing to them. How can you administer justice when all sense of reason has gone? It is not that I disbelieve the supernatural, but I believe passionately in justice, and in the protection of the innocent. I do not much care if the wicked go free—their evil deeds will catch them up. It matters far more that the innocent shall not be punished. To me, in this "hunt", it will not be the victim alone that I must defend from ignorance and passion. Justice itself will be on trial, and I shall be responsible for keeping it in honour.

But I must not burden you with my troubles. Philippa, my daughter, will you tell Cook that we shall have a visitor from tonight, and that he will be here for supper. And where is Mistress Alice? She should know too. His room must be prepared.

PHILIPPA

A visitor, Father! Who is it? I suppose it's only the Archdeacon again.

SIR MARTIN

I wish it were. It is the King's Agent come down from London to lead the witch-hunt. As I am one of the Justices, I am expected to entertain him. He won't find me helpful to his cause.

PHILIPPA

Have you seen him? What is he like?

BESS

He'll be some old legal fogey. You needn't be so bright-eyed. He's some rheumy old man with bent knees, isn't he, Father? With a drop on the end of his nose. Look at Philippa! She thinks she's going to get married right away!

PHILIPPA

Little beast!

SIR MARTIN

You are silly girls. But you are at the silly age. He is, for a job like this, the worst, the most ruthless type of man there could be—young, ambitious, with his name to make.

PHILIPPA AND BESS

He's young! He's ambitious! (*They start to dance a jig.*)
(*Together*) I wonder if he is handsome. (*They link little fingers and wish.*)

SIR MARTIN

Where is Mistress Alice?

PHILIPPA

I expect she's in the still-room as usual. She was making cough syrup ready for the colds we are going to have. And skin-lotion for our hands. Mine are so red.

SIR MARTIN

Go and tell her, Philippa. And Bess, will you please tell Cook. I must take off these muddy clothes. (*Exit up right.*)

(*Jenny goes up into the gallery with her dog Fido. Philippa and Bess cut high-spirited capers.*)

PHILIPPA AND BESS

A visitor! A stranger! A young man! An ambitious young man!

BESS

He may be a hunchback. Or as ugly as a toad.

PHILIPPA

I do hope he'll be handsome. I hope he's handsome and romantic.

(*Enter down left from kitchen, Walter with Old Mother Alison Taylor, followed by Cook. Walter puts a stool in front of fire and exits, Fido barks.*)

COOK

Sit yourself there, Old Mother, and warm yourself up. Why, you're wet through! I saw those boys plaguing you. They've no respect for age.

OLD MOTHER

That's a fine fire! That's good!

(*Philippa and Bess sidle forward arm in arm to stare at the old woman. She gets to her feet to curtsy, knocking over the stool.*)

OLD MOTHER

God bless you, young ladies.

(*They back away and Bess puts her handkerchief to her nose while she speaks.*)

BESS

Father says he is having a very important visitor for supper tonight and you are to prepare a very special meal.

COOK

Very well, young ladies. But I shall need some stores from Mistress Alice. Here you are, Gammer, something to warm your old bones. Sit down to it.

PHILIPPA

I'm going to tell her now. And you'd better get your old grandmother out of the way before the visitor comes, too.

COOK

She can sit there awhile, no one will come yet. She's in no one's way. Look how she trembles. (*She turns her back to set down the pan of soup. As the girls turn to go, Bess hooks away the stool with her foot and the old woman falls, spilling her soup.*) There! Look what you've done. I can't go on heating up soup for you now that I'm busy.

(*The girls laugh; Philippa exits to still-room, Bess goes to sit on the stairs.*)

Cook

There's still some hot in the pan. Take care this time. No good will come to those two young ladies. They are a wild, proud pair.

(*Re-enter Philippa and joins Bess on the stairs.*)

Bess

What a pestilential old thing. She must have been sleeping in farmyards. I say, what if she's a witch? She looks like one. What would happen if she were? Why did you tell Cook to send her away? The visitor might have been pleased. She might be the first catch of the season.

Philippa

I don't want him getting on his hobby-horse the minute he arrives. I want him to have time to notice me.

Bess

Us.

Philippa

You're too young. Me.

Bess

I think I'm quite as pretty as you are. My teeth are smaller. And I can make a dimple. Like this.

Philippa

Then you wouldn't be able to talk. Or kiss.

Bess

Oh mercy! Kiss whom?

PHILIPPA

Who knows?

BESS

The Parson! (*Laughter.*)

PHILIPPA

The Parson! (*Hysterics of laughter.*)

BESS

I say, there's Father's little sweetheart, his little inno-cent. How about telling her there's a witch in front of the fire?

(*They suck in their lips over their teeth and make clawing signs, and nod to each other.*)

PHILIPPA

Sweetheart!

BESS

Mousie, mousie, mousie, mousie!

JENNY

What is it? (*They crouch for her, whispering.*)

PHILIPPA

Sh! Something very frightening has happened. I'm shak-ing with fear. We must warn you about it, because you are such a trustful innocent.

BESS

Sh! Be careful, Philippa, she might hear.

PHILIPPA

Oh, do you think . . . . Jenny, down there, she's a witch. She has no teeth and hands like claws.

BESS

She looks like the Devil himself, crouching there all in black. I thought I saw him peep out from under her skirts. That's why I tipped up her stool, to see if he would run out.

PHILIPPA

He went up the chimney. Devils are used to fire.

JENNY

(*after a moment of alarm, laughs*)

You're making it up to frighten me. It's only the old woman you were throwing things at. (*Enter Walter down right, pauses.*)

BESS

Because she's a witch. We wanted her to go away, not to come here. But Father would bring her in.

PHILIPPA

Even after what she did to him.

JENNY

What did she do to him?

BESS

She made the Sign of the Cross with her bare legs in the air. That's very wicked. Only witches do that.

Philippa

To make his horse shy and throw him. He might have broken his neck. (*Exit Walter centre back.*)

Jenny

Oh no!

Philippa

Just come and peep at her. You'll see. She's a horribly old thing, with the Evil Eye. (*They drag Jenny downstairs and push her forward. The old woman is dozing and warming her bare shins.*)

Jenny

Good evening, Old Mother. Are you warmer now?

Old Mother

God bless you, little love. Sitting here I'm as warm as a queen. Keep your dog away, little lady. I've neither shoes nor hose if he should bite.

Philippa

(*pulling Jenny away*)

Come away, you little fool. She's put the Evil Eye on your precious Fido.

Jenny

She hasn't!

Bess

She did. I saw it. And she pointed too. After all, Fido did bark when she came in. Good dog, Fido, good dog! He knew.

PHILIPPA

Good dog! (*They both scamper upstairs laughing and exit via gallery, left. After a long pause Jenny comes forward again.*)

JENNY

Old Mother, I know it's nice and warm here, but go away. (*Enter Cook.*) Please go away quickly, now.

COOK

Why, my dear, what's the matter? That behaviour is not like you. It's unkind.

JENNY

I'm frightened.

COOK

What of, lovely? You've nothing to be frightened of.

JENNY

But I am. For her. And for Father too.

COOK

For your Father! What have you got in your little head!

JENNY

Tell her to go, Cook. My sisters may make mischief.

OLD MOTHER
(*resignedly*)

I'll go, little lady. Thank you, ma'am, for the soup. It's a lovely fire to leave. (*Exit left.*)

COOK

Mischief's quickly done as I know. And a great satisfaction to those that do it. I don't suppose she had anywhere to go, either.

JENNY

What will she do?

COOK

I don't know, I'm sure, poor thing.

JENNY

I'm sorry. (*She goes to window and presses herself in the window-seat.*)

(*Enter Alice, from still-room. She is young, big, handsome, with a face like a pale mask. She is remote and makes no pretension to be part of the family. As housekeeper she goes in and out of the rooms at will, walking superbly and checking to listen or glance now and then. She laughs briefly, but never smiles, except once. She now stands, centre, with a large bunch of keys, and moves her head, questing like an animal. Her voice is low, sexy but offhand.*)

ALICE

I sense a stirring of evil.

CURTAIN

SCENE II

The girls' bedroom.

Alice dressing Philippa's hair. Bess looking on.

PHILIPPA

Just fancy—a young gentleman from London! We never see anything but old men. Just because Mother died, Father needn't make us all live like hermits. It's two years now, and we've hardly met a young man since last year's skating. I thought when my brother Francis went to Cambridge he would bring his friends for hunting or coursing. You would think so. But with Father so sober and gloomy I suppose it is more fun anywhere else. We have to stay mewed up here, in old-fashioned clothes and not knowing the new way to talk. You sound like a fool if you don't know it.

ALICE

Frowning spoils your face, Philippa. And it is never wise to show your feelings. You have a great advantage over other people if they have no idea what you think. You must learn to wear your face—not just to have it. You could practise even here. For instance, it would be difficult to fox Bess. You could have fun that way. It would be quite an art. Your Father would be easy enough, but your manner to him so far would deceive nobody. Roll your eyes up, Philippa. I'll put some drops in to brighten them.

PHILIPPA

Ow!

ALICE

There. Look up at me now. Oh. Swimming with tears and very fetching. It takes a moment or two to stop smarting.

PHILIPPA

I have put on my new point lace collar. Is it right?

ALICE

First you can sit here with your hands in this bowl. They need softening. Your turn, Bess.

PHILIPPA

Isn't she too young to be dressed up?

ALICE

She's old enough to be married.

PHILIPPA

She!!

ALICE

Scowling again. You are a bad pupil. She is very pretty. (*Philippa smirks.*) That's better. I see you are learning.

BESS

Am I prettier than she is?

ALICE

(*She watches Philippa who changes to an arrogant who-cares smile. Alice laughs.*)

What a question. Every pretty girl, if she is clever, surrounds herself with other pretty girls, so that the young man she wants will enjoy himself among so many, and still see that she is the most attractive.

PHILIPPA AND BESS

(*Looking at each other*)

Oh.

ALICE

It needs self-control, and no scowling. Change places with Philippa, Bess. Now, Philippa, let me see to that collar. Good. Lastly, some of my muckrose perfume on your neck and bosom. There. And some for Bess.

PHILIPPA

Oh, no!

ALICE

Now, now!

PHILIPPA

But we can't both smell exactly alike. That would be too ridiculous.

ALICE

It would rather. Bess can have violet oil.

BESS

Ooh! Don't I smell lovely!

ALICE

Now you are both ready. I can't do any more. See what you can do.

PHILIPPA

Do you think he will talk to us? What shall we say to him?

ALICE

Something he might like to hear. If you can think of anything. It sounds as if he has arrived. We will go down. All set?

The scene changes to the ante-room.

(Movements of servants, sounds of horses and arrivals. Sir Martin comes into the ante-room from centre back, holding Jenny by the hand. Alice, Philippa and Bess come down stairs and stand left.)

WALTER

Mr. Simon Upjohn.

(Enter Mr. Upjohn, right. He is a brutally handsome teenage idol, ultra fashionable in black with bold eyes and very flexible manners. He wears a red ribbon garter on his right leg and a black on his left. Colours reversed on his wrists. Walter takes his cloak and hat.)

SIR MARTIN

Welcome to our house, Mr. Upjohn. We cannot entertain you in the London style, but please make the best of our country comforts.

UPJOHN

I am greatly honoured.

SIR MARTIN

I hope your journey was good?

UPJOHN

Do not take it personally if I say the roads in your county are abominably muddy and pot-holed, and even under water for a long stretch. But we met with no robbers on the way and I did not need my sword.

(Unbuckles it and hands it to Walter. Exit Walter.)

SIR MARTIN

We don't anticipate robbers here. We are too far from the London road. Now, Mr. Upjohn, this is my youngest daughter, Jenny. (*She curtsies.*)

UPJOHN

A pretty child. (*He tries to chuck her under the chin, but she backs away to her father.*)

And clearly, from the way she clings to you, your favourite.

SIR MARTIN

I am sorry if I let it be seen so clearly. She resembles her dear mother, whom I have lost.

UPJOHN

(*bowing*)

My condolences.

SIR MARTIN

My son is not here. He is studying law at Cambridge. My eldest daughter, Philippa. (*Upjohn bows, she curtsies and then naïvely holds out her hand. He kisses it, she wriggles.*)

UPJOHN

Court manners for a young lady who would grace St. James's.

PHILIPPA

(*genteelly*)

Are you much at Court, sir?

Upjohn

Do not make fun of me, charming Mistress Philippa. I am in the Courts every day, pursuing his August Majesty the Devil, which is my calling. For this reason, I often have cause to wait upon His Majesty King James, who takes a keen interest. In his ante-chamber one may wait for hours, but the time is pleasantly spent as persons of the highest rank are waiting too. There is a great exchange of compliment and interest.

Philippa

Fancy that, Bess!

Sir Martin

My younger daughter, Bess.

Upjohn

So this is Bess. She is perhaps not yet too old to be saluted on the cheek. (*Kisses her.*) A visiting friend is always somewhat in the position of an uncle.

(*The two girls glare at each other, with grins, and Bess makes her dimple.*)

Had I known that I was coming into so charming a family of young girls, I would have tried to bring each a little gift from London. As it is, I have only brought His Majesty's learned book on witchcraft, which I would like to offer you, Sir, if you don't already possess it.

Sir Martin

You are most kind. This lady is my housekeeper, Mistress Alice.

(*They salute each other off-handedly.*)

Come, Mr. Upjohn, sit down. Let me offer you a tankard

of mulled ale until supper is ready. Walter! Bring some mulled ale. (*To Jenny.*) My pet, go and sit with your sisters.

UPJOHN

I must apologise for the length of time I may have to trouble your hospitality. I will do my best to get His Majesty's business done as quickly as possible.

SIR MARTIN

It is an honour to entertain the King's emissary. And justice cannot be hurried.

(*Enter Walter with tankards.*)

WALTER

May I offer some to Mr. Upjohn's Secretary who is in the servants' hall?

SIR MARTIN

Of course, of course. I do not think you will find much devilry in or around our quiet country town. It is a prosperous law-abiding district. Neighbourly folk.

UPJOHN

I am afraid you may be rudely awakened. Human nature is the same all the world over, and my little investigation will be like a miniature Day of Judgement. There is nothing hid that shall not be made known and the secrets of all hearts shall be revealed.

SIR MARTIN

There have been no accusations, nor have I heard any rumours of witchcraft for years.

UPJOHN

The accusations will come. The very fact that there is an investigation of witchcraft proves that there are witches to be examined.

SIR MARTIN

No, sir. It does not.

UPJOHN

(*laughing*)

Of course it does not. But people will think it does. Everyone who has ever injured anyone—and your innocent country folk are not above a dirty trick now and again—will remember some unexplained accident to themselves that could have been revenge, and the sick will think of someone who could be sitting watching a candle burn down and willing them to die as it goes out. And as the snowball grows, everyone will begin to remember the Devil whom all fear in their hearts more than God. And then every tongue will be loosed. Oh, there will be accusations enough.

(*Enter Walter with a note.*)

WALTER

Your Secretary asked that I would deliver this to you, sir.

UPJOHN

(*continuing*)

Accusations enough. And everyone will believe them. Excuse me, Sir Martin.

(*Opens, reads, writes a few words.*) Ask him to see to that right away.

(*Exit Walter.*)

Sir Martin

I should be very grieved to see trouble and back-biting among my neighbours, or among those who serve me.

Upjohn

Yes, I am sure. And there's the family circle to think of too. Very disturbing. It is usually their relatives that people hate or fear most. You, of course, cannot fear that. What a charming group they make! But the Devil nudges in where he can.

Sir Martin

I wonder, Mr. Upjohn, if your method of working does not aid him more than it hinders, and leave the world worse than it was.

Upjohn

Unfortunately, my fish is only caught in troubled waters. You must admit that it is a man's first business to do thoroughly what he has undertaken. To do myself justice, I get results. And from what I see in the course of my investigation, the world could hardly be worse than it is.

(*Enter Walter, centre back.*)

Walter

Supper is served, Sir. (*Exit.*)

Sir Martin

Come, Mr. Upjohn. Shall I lead the way?

(*Upjohn steps back and motions to Philippa to go first. He bows as she goes past. She is embarrassed and drops half a curtsy. Bess follows with saucy looks. Jenny gets a sweeping iconic bow and runs past. Alice and Upjohn stand face to face for a deep look. She throws her head back and smiles.*)

He makes in the air the Sign of the Cross backward [right-left, down-up] quickly, as if he were shaking back the lace of his cuff. She gives a long reverential curtsy and kisses his red garter.)

ALICE

Grand Master! My Lord!
(*She precedes him to exit.*)

CURTAIN

Scene III

The ante-room. Next morning.

Philippa and Bess on the gallery, arms on each other's shoulders, looking down.

PHILIPPA

I wonder if he's up yet. I would think he would get up early. He's so vital.

BESS

Wasn't it a change last night from watching Father and the Vicar playing chess. Mr. Upjohn laughs so well—you have to laugh with him.

PHILIPPA

He laughed enough at your playing your little piece on the lute.

BESS

That was because I was pulling faces at him.

PHILIPPA

It was fun singing madrigals. A tenor voice comes creeping up my spine somehow. He kept looking at me in "Love do not deny me".

BESS

That was to try to keep you on the right note.

PHILIPPA

Pig! You are jealous.

BESS

Nothing to be jealous of.

PHILIPPA

That's all you know!

BESS

What, then?

PHILIPPA

Well, I told him about the old woman yesterday. I thought he would like to know. He said some very complimentary things to me afterwards.

BESS

You do think you are Somebody. I told him too.

PHILIPPA

You did! When?

BESS

When we were looking through the sheets of music. Looking for "Love do not deny me", no doubt.

PHILIPPA

What did he say to you?

BESS

Wouldn't you like to know! Sh! (*They take up elegant attitudes over the stair rail. Enter below Sir Martin and Mr. Upjohn, back. At the same time Walter admits the Secretary at entrance right.*)

UPJOHN

I was sorry to hear, Sir, that your horse threw you yesterday. I hope you were feeling no ill effects while you were entertaining me. Is there much stiffness this morning? (*To Secretary.*) Good day.

SIR MARTIN

Good day, Mr. Secretary. (*They walk on.*) Who told you about my fall? It was not worth mentioning. My horse shied and his hind feet slipped in the mud. I simply rolled off on to soft ground. It was nothing.

UPJOHN

I am glad to hear it. You were fortunate. What caused your horse to shy, at the end of a long journey, at his own gate?

SIR MARTIN

The unexpected sight of an old woman lying in the ditch, poor old thing.

UPJOHN

I am glad to have your own voluntary statement. Make a note of that, Mr. Secretary.

SIR MARTIN

What sort of procedure is this? I am making no statement to you. I am in my own house talking, as I thought, to a guest. Explain yourself and the presence of your unwanted Secretary.

UPJOHN

Forgive my little stratagem. If we were in a court of law I could hardly question the justice. But a voluntary statement from you could have a good effect. After all, what have you said? That your horse shied at an old woman in a ditch. The barest statement that could be made, and of unquestionable truth. The barest statement! Quite amusing. I am told her bare legs were waving in the air.

SECRETARY

Ha ha!

UPJOHN

You are not in a court of law now. Kindly behave with proper respect.

SIR MARTIN
(*to Secretary*)

Get out of here at once. (*Exit Secretary.*) It is an outrage.

UPJOHN

As for the second part of your protest, my dear host, that I was not behaving like a guest—if an accusation is made by a member of your own household, I assume you would prefer the preliminary sifting to be done with as much privacy as possible?

SIR MARTIN

What you suggest is hideous. I cannot accept it.

UPJOHN

I told you the accusations would come.
(*The girls shrink out of sight.*)

SIR MARTIN
(*sitting down heavily*)

Who in my household has accused whom?

Upjohn

Come now, come now! Such a weight of discouragement will put ideas into my head! Our business only concerns a wandering stranger—a mere beggar.

Sir Martin

If anyone in my household has borne false witness against a stranger or anyone else, rich or poor, I will see to it that they suffer the full rigour of the law. There is a penalty for false witness. There is nothing angers me so absolutely as trumped-up charges.

Upjohn

It becomes you. You look like Jove himself. But swearing to a reasonable suspicion is not perjury, even if it prove unfounded. As it rarely does, witchcraft being so wide-spread.

Sir Martin

God have mercy on us all! Idle chatter from the servants, I suppose. I thought better of them all.

Upjohn

Idle chatter is the natural relief of servants. And its best spice is repetition of what is said in here.

Sir Martin

What! What are you hinting?

Upjohn

You yourself sent the old woman in here. Shall we call in Walter?

SIR MARTIN

Walter? He's not been here long. Still hardly more than a boy. But a good one, or so I thought. I will hear what Walter has to say, but I will question him myself.

UPJOHN

Certainly. Certainly.

SIR MARTIN

Walter!

(*Enter Walter.*)

Come here, boy. Now, Walter, you have not been with me long, but I know your parents well and I think well of you. I believe you tell the truth, and you must tell it now.

WALTER

Yes, Sir.

SIR MARTIN

What is this story you have been repeating in the kitchen, accusing that poor old woman of witchcraft—about whom none of us know anything, either good or bad, except that she seems destitute?

WALTER

I didn't accuse anybody, honestly, Sir. I only repeated in the servants' hall what Mistress Philippa and her sister said. We always repeat what the young ladies say. It makes for laughter and conversation. And it was funny, what she said.

SIR MARTIN

Go on, boy. What did she say?

WALTER

Mistress Philippa said the old woman was a witch and had made your horse throw you on purpose, and you might have been killed.

SIR MARTIN

That was found laughable in the kitchen?

WALTER

No, Sir. But Mistress Bess said the witch lay on her back and made the Sign of the Cross with her bare legs in the air. I . . . I thought that was funny, Sir.

UPJOHN

It's always unwise to laugh at the Devil, boy.

WALTER

It wouldn't have been funny if it was true, Sir, but it was little Mistress Bess saying a thing like that.

SIR MARTIN

Bess too! You were not there, Walter, when my horse shied. You met me only after I had given my horse to the groom. The old woman had fallen on her back, head downwards in the ditch, pushed, I am afraid, by some boys. Robert Bell and his lot. If her legs were in the air that was because she couldn't help it and was trying to right herself. Do you understand that?

WALTER

Yes, Sir.

SIR MARTIN

I see. I am sure you never meant the harm you have done, but to prevent worse, I charge you never to alter the simple truth of your story. It puts the blame, I know, on my daughters, who were guilty of almost unforgivable folly, but not on the old woman who was guilty of nothing.

WALTER

Yes, Sir.

SIR MARTIN

Now go and call my two elder daughters.
(*Walter goes up to the bedroom door.*)

WALTER

Mistress Philippa, Mistress Bess!

PHILIPPA AND BESS

What is it, Walter?

WALTER

Your Father wants to speak to you both.

BESS

Does he look angry?

WALTER

Very stern, Mistress Bess.

PHILIPPA

Oh, dear! Now for it. Come on, then, Bess. We are too old to be beaten. At least I am. After all, we only said what we thought.
(*They go down, reluctantly, and curtsy to both men. Exit Walter.*)

Sir Martin

Come here, my daughters. I am very greatly displeased with what I hear about your wanton, unfounded talk yesterday afternoon. You are reported to have said that a harmless old woman was a witch. Did you make such an accusation?

(*The girls look in consternation at Upjohn, who smiles deprecatingly.*)

Upjohn

Young ladies, please forgive my presence at a moment of parental displeasure, which would normally be private. In my capacity as Prosecutor I must be present when this little matter is cleared up.

Sir Martin

What have you to say for yourselves?

(*Silence.*)

Do you admit having said such a—thing?

Philippa

— — — — Yes, Father.

Bess

Yes, Father.

Upjohn

I see you have two truthful girls, who would not alter their story to suit the hearer.

Sir Martin

To whom did you tell this monstrous story?

BOTH

To Jenny.

SIR MARTIN

Why? Why did you say this cruel thing to a trusting child?

PHILIPPA

To warn her, because she is so trusting.

SIR MARTIN

Were you not teasing her, as you often do?

BOTH

Oh no, Father.

SIR MARTIN

You were making stories up for play?

PHILIPPA

No, Father.

SIR MARTIN

But you had absolutely no reason for thinking the old woman was a witch. Don't tell me about her poor old legs.

PHILIPPA

I saw her shake her fist at the house. And then afterwards she made your horse throw you.

(*Upjohn nods approval. Enter Alice on gallery left; seen only by Upjohn.*)

BESS

And then Jenny's precious Fido barked at the old woman, and she pointed at him and cast the Evil Eye on him, and Jenny went away crying.

(*Bess looks at Upjohn for approval, but only gets an ironic look.*)

SIR MARTIN

And has anything happened to Fido?

BESS

No, not yet.

(*Alice nods. Exit Alice.*)

SIR MARTIN

Not yet! Oh, in the name of God, you weary me with your malicious, ignorant nonsense. What can one do in such a quicksand of irresponsible folly? You have started the Devil's work. Do you understand that this old creature will have to suffer all the ordeals—which prove nothing either way, but may result in her being hanged though innocent? Go to your room and stay there till you come to your senses. You disgrace me. Don't think I shall temper the law for you. It is not too late to confess that you were inventing stories for some idiotic satisfaction of your own. You are not under oath yet. But you will be. Go.

(*Exeunt Philippa and Bess upstairs. Sir Martin paces about in a fury while Upjohn sits swinging his gartered leg.*)

This is adolescent hysteria. At their age girls are the most irrational, irritating creatures. You really would think sometimes the Devil was in them. But it means nothing—nothing. I beg you, sir, for God's sake, not for mine, dismiss this as the nonsense it is.

UPJOHN

I regret, Sir Martin, it has gone too far already. When my Secretary sent me word last night, I started enquiries. The old woman is already in custody. The case must be brought. I have no doubt that with you, Sir, on the bench, she will have a fair trial. But even should she be acquitted, she will have startled the neighbourhood into a more profitable state of terror. We need a climate of suspicion.

SIR MARTIN

Allow me to tell you, sir, that you are an exceedingly wicked man.

UPJOHN

(jovially)

No offence taken. Personal opinions are allowed. You, Sir, were trying to influence witness.

SIR MARTIN

They are my daughters, even if I am a Justice.

UPJOHN

I'm not objecting. I don't object, because if they are afraid of you—as they obviously are—such an awe-inspiring display of wrath as you have just given will only make them cling to their story. By so doing at least they save their importance. If they retract, they are reduced to naughty children. Their best hope is for me to win the case.

Dare I say, so early in the game, Check!

CURTAIN

Scene IV

The girls' bedroom and the ante-room.

BESS

Oh dear! We have got ourselves into trouble now. I've never seen Father in such a rage.

PHILIPPA

He didn't say much, but he was in a rage all right. I don't see why that smelly old ragbag matters so much—more than his own daughters. You can see he's not going to do anything to save our faces. How could we say we had made it all up when we had both said it to Mr. Upjohn? I only said it to make conversation. Alice told us to say anything that would interest him.

BESS

It's a good thing we have Mr. Upjohn on our side.

PHILIPPA

Do you think that? It is true he didn't give us away. I mean, he didn't say we had told him.

BESS

It's more than that. He needs us. We are in it together.

PHILIPPA

You are bright for your age, Bess. (*Dreamily.*) We could help his career.

BESS

He will be very splendid in Court. All the girls will be watching him, and see us there talking to him. He'll have to be rather special with us, because we don't have to do it. If we went back on it he would look a fool.

PHILIPPA

He'll never do that. But he is bound to be grateful to us. Nothing Father can threaten will make me go back on it now.

BESS

You'll be a martyr for love, I suppose.

PHILIPPA

All the same, it will be frightening with Father sitting there in glory. What if Father is cleverer than he is?

BESS

Father isn't clever. He's only old and respected.

PHILIPPA

Father's sent for Francis to come from Cambridge and defend her. They will make quite a strong side, both being local too. It will be two against one. And Francis is very good-looking.

BESS

Two against three.

PHILIPPA

Don't exaggerate your own importance, you silly. Why ever did you say that about the old creature putting the Evil Eye on Fido? You only did it to get into the conversation.

BESS

You call it conversation, with Father in a rage like that? I had to say something.

PHILIPPA

But Fido is perfectly well. After all, the horse shied before
we said so.
(*They start giggling and then laugh wildly.*)

BESS

(*imitating her father*)

"A quicksand of irresponsible folly." Poor Father. He really
minds.
(*Enter Alice.*)

ALICE

You sound quite merry.

PHILIPPA AND BESS TOGETHER

What have you brought? Oh, dry bread and milk again.

BESS

Nothing else?

ALICE

Nothing else.

BESS

What are you having downstairs?

ALICE

Trout. Roast wild boar and glazed apples.

BOTH

Oooh!

ALICE

Pigeon pie, sherry syllabub.

BOTH

Oooh!

ALICE

Peaches in brandy.

BESS

Oh, it's too bad. Will Francis be there?

ALICE

He will be.

BESS

How long have we got to stay here?

ALICE

Till repentance or till after the trial—except for your appearance at it, of course.

PHILIPPA

Is it like a funeral, or do we wear our best clothes?

ALICE

It is more like a party. Everyone who is "appearing"—except the prisoner, of course—makes the best im-pression they can.

PHILIPPA

Hooray! Not that our best is very good. Could I be making new rosettes for my shoes? Look at them, they are crushed. Can I have some ribbon?

BESS

How's Fido?

ALICE

Fido? He's very frisky. Why do you ask?

BESS

I'm not nervous about the trial, not really, except about this Fido business. He's too well.

ALICE

You should have thought of that before.

BESS

How long does the Evil Eye take to work?

ALICE

Days. Weeks. Months. But in this case unless it works before the trial tomorrow it will be no help to you. The first part of your story is feeble enough, and the second part feebler. I'll get you the ribbon, Philippa. Your brother may make you look a fool at the trial, but at least you can show a pretty foot.

(*Exit Alice, via gallery.*)

PHILIPPA

Francis! Why does this have to be such a family affair? He knows too much about us. A brother isn't fair.

(*They sit sulking with their elbows on the table.*)

PHILIPPA

(*screams*)

Dominos! (*She thumps them with her fist, hurts herself and cries.*)

BESS

I've got an idea.

PHILIPPA

What?

BESS

It's rather naughty.

PHILIPPA

Naughty! How old do you think you are?

BESS

I do have that sort of feeling about it. But it can't be helped now. It won't do any real harm.

(*Re-enter Alice, via gallery left.*)

ALICE

Here are your ribbons, Philippa. That will keep you busy for a while. I'll take the tray down now.

BESS

I haven't finished my milk. Don't rush away. We're tired of being alone. I want to talk to you.

ALICE

I'm busy downstairs. I can't stay.

BESS

Well, bring Fido up then. He's better than nothing. I am so bored.

(*Alice makes as if to go.*)

Wait, wait. And I need some of your physic. I think I need a good strong dose.

140

ALICE

Do you think so? Very well. I'll bring Fido and the physic. (*Goes downstairs and exits by still-room.*)

PHILIPPA

So that's what you are going to do.

BESS

It won't hurt him. We take it ourselves. But his symptoms will certainly be noticed. Imagine the inter-rupted supper party! Quick, quick!! (*They laugh.*)
It's a good thing we can laugh.

PHILIPPA

I hear horses. It must be Francis arriving. (*They rush to the window, right.*) Yes, there he is.

BESS

And Father.

PHILIPPA

And Mr. Upjohn!!

BESS

Doesn't Father look shabby beside them? Francis is really stylish in a quiet sort of way.

PHILIPPA

But not like Mr. Upjohn.

BESS

Oh no. Not like him!

PHILIPPA

I wish we were downstairs. Shut up here and made to look like children in his eyes. I can't bear it.

(*Re-enter Alice. She runs upstairs with Fido under her arm.*)

ALICE

Here's Fido. And your physic, Bess. I brought two in case Philippa wanted one as well. Take it in milk. I must run. Francis is here. I'll be back later.

BESS

Don't be long.

(*Alice starts down the stairs.*)

BESS

Come on, Fido. Come to be made a fuss of. You've got to have some physic, do you know?

PHILIPPA

One's enough. We might have to give him some more to-morrow. I'll put the other in this box, see? Here. We'll say we each had one.

BESS

Bring the milk. Now then, Fido, be a good dog. (*They dose him.*) There. Good dog. All gone. Wipe his whiskers, Philippa, he's all milky. Poor Fido. You've had physic before. It's only gripes.

(*Sits with Fido on her lap. Party sounds downstairs. Enter Walter from centre back, Sir Martin, Upjohn, Francis, Jenny from entrance right.*)

Sir Martin

It is good to have you here, my dear boy. You have wasted no time. I am most unhappy about this affair.

Francis

I know you are, Father. I am afraid Mr. Upjohn must think you have called in a very inexperienced opponent for him.

Sir Martin

You must not underrate him, Mr. Upjohn. Though he is young, he brings from Cambridge a brilliant reputation.

Upjohn

We will cross swords with all the more pleasure when the time comes.

Francis

(*to Jenny*)

Well, my sweet little ha'porth, why do I only get half a welcome? Where's the other half of the penny, Fido? I expect a whirl of welcome from him.

Jenny

I thought he was here. Where *is* Fido? Fido!

Alice

(*curtsying to Francis*)

I'll get him, Jenny. I saw him in the kitchen just now. (*Exit left.*)

Sir Martin

Come on through into the hall, all of you. Come, Jenny. (*Exeunt centre back.*)

(*Girls' bedroom. Enter Alice from gallery left.*)

ALICE

Finished with the physic and Fido? Jenny's calling for him. I'll take him.

(*Exit left.*)

BESS

Did she know?

CURTAIN

SCENE V

The ante-room. Next morning.

Sir Martin, Francis, Kennelman, Alice and Jenny bending over Fido.

KENNELMAN

That warn't no distemper, Sir. 'Twas poison. Couldn't be anything else with those symptoms.

SIR MARTIN

Where would he get it? He's always fed in the house. Jenny sees to him herself.

JENNY

Is he dead, Alice?

ALICE

Yes. Oh yes. He's dead. (*Holds him up by back legs like a rabbit.*)

JENNY

Poor F— F— F— (*Bursts into tears and runs to her father.*)

KENNELMAN

Poor little maid!

FRANCIS

Could the old woman have done it?

SIR MARTIN

In God's name, I hope not. Jenny, my darling, control yourself. Look up, there, there. Tell me, sweetheart, did the old woman give him anything to eat?

JENNY

Nooooo.

KENNELMAN

It will be the Evil Eye, like Miss Bess said.

SIR MARTIN

So everyone will say. But saying nonsense doesn't make it true. Have you been buying ratbane from any of those pedlars?

KENNELMAN

No, Sir. It's too dangerous.

SIR MARTIN

Come, my love. You shall have another Fido just like him, and you'll love him just as much.

(*Jenny continues crying.*)

Mistress Alice, the Kennelman will take him away. Do you go please and see that those shameless girls are ready in time.

(*Exeunt Alice and Kennelman.*)

FRANCIS

This will make my defence much more difficult. You see the Kennelman is half convinced already.

SIR MARTIN

The people you have to convince are the other three Justices. They can outvote me.

FRANCIS

What are they likely to think?

Sir Martin

Girth will agree with everybody all the way through. If the crowd shout to save her he will join them. But I greatly fear they will shout for her execution. She is a stranger, you see. If you could persuade Girth, we should be even numbers and the trial would at least be postponed. Of the other two, Fever is a superstitious fellow. He fears everything and the Evil Eye most. De Groot believes that a Justice is there to condemn everyone regardless. The Prosecutor will do what he likes with those two, but the crowd has some influence.

Francis

You seem to have brought me here in the certainty that I must fail.

Sir Martin

You will find that is the normal situation of anyone talking simple sense when passions have been worked up. If you can keep a breath of cool common sense alive in the Court and even a little decency, we might possibly get her acquitted. It won't be easy. You may even begin to wonder whether to be sane and just is not the only real madness. But at least this time I shall know there are two of us.

Francis

Thank you, Father.

Sir Martin

And you, Jenny, you're one of us. Come, wipe your eyes. Let's go and see Francis's new horse. Bring an apple for him.

(*Exeunt right.*)

(Enter Upjohn centre back, and Alice descending the stairs. She curtsies.)

UPJOHN

This was your doing?

ALICE

No, my Lord. I work with more subtlety than that. I let the young ladies think of it themselves and do it themselves. And more will come of it, for they will know how to use it and will see how useful it is.

UPJOHN

Are you planning that they shall be the next accused? What would their most honourable father do then?

ALICE

Hang them, I should think. They are quite out of favour. His precious Jenny would be a better target, but even you, my Lord, would never make anyone believe it of her. Forgive me for doubting your powers. But the girls are well away. That dim-wit Philippa will gaze at you in Court like a dog drooling at the food on its master's plate. Sh!

(She starts and runs halfway up stairs. Exit Upjohn centre.)

CURTAIN

Scene VI

The girls' bedroom.
Philippa and Bess within.

PHILIPPA

Yesterday I was so excited about today. Something going on for once, all the neighbours coming. I thought it would be like a play.

BESS

With Mr. Upjohn as the leading man and you as the leading lady.

PHILIPPA

Well, he will be there, that's certain. But I feel so worked up and shaky. Don't you?

BESS

Yes. I feel frightened. I don't know why. (*Enter Alice.*) Oh, at last! What was all the commotion about down-stairs?

ALICE

Jenny was crying about Fido.

BESS

Isn't he well today?

ALICE

He's dead. The Kennelman said he was poisoned.
(*Shocked silence.*)

BESS

But I thought — — — — we thought — —

ALICE

You Both thought the old witch had put the Evil Eye on him.

(*Silence.*)

Well, she must have done, mustn't she? So, really you don't have to worry about the trial any more. The case is proved. Now, come along. Get ready.

BESS

What will they do to the old woman?

ALICE

Everything they can think of.

BESS

Oh, Father will stop them.

ALICE

He won't be able to. How are your shoes, Philippa? Show me.

PHILIPPA

(*posturing*)

Do I stand like this? Or like this?

(*While they are busy, Bess looks quickly in the box.*)

BESS

(*aside*)

It's gone! Which of them has it? It's dangerous.

ALICE

What's the matter, Bess? Aren't you feeling well? You haven't got gripes, have you, after that physic? (*Shakes her.*) Have you?

BESS

I'm all right now. Where's my kerchief?

PHILIPPA

(*still posturing*)

My shoes look really quite taking. I am going to enjoy myself after all. Being asked questions by him and always giving him the answer he wants seems somehow rather like a love scene.

CURTAIN

ACT II

The Court Room in Sir Martin's house. The Justices' rostrum centre back. Below, Clerk, Prosecutor and Counsel.

Witnesses (Philippa, Bess, Jenny, five boys), right.

Parson, Physician, Mayor, left.

Dock down left. Crowds on gallery and stairs.

Witch Searcher, Witch Pricker, Constables and Old Mother Alison Taylor wait extreme left.

(All stand as Justices enter.)

Justice Fever
(*to Girth*)

They say at night the witches dance with the Devil himself and that he roars like a bull. There's no decent word for the goings-on.

Justice Girth

Well, your dancing days are over anyway. And mine!

Justice de Groot

We'll burn them out, root and branch. It's the only way.

(Justices take their seats.)

Sir Martin

Bring in the accused.

(*Alison Taylor, obviously the worse for rough treatment, is led forward by Witch Searcher and Witch Pricker.*)

CLERK

Alison Taylor, you stand accused of witchcraft in that on the afternoon of January twelfth you did by making an obscene sign cause the horse of Sir Martin Westbury to throw him, whereby he might have been killed, and that afterwards in his house you did cast the Evil Eye upon his daughter's dog and caused it to die. How say you, are you guilty or not guilty?

OLD MOTHER

I done nothing.

SIR MARTIN

Alison Taylor, have you anything you wish to say?

OLD MOTHER

Yes, Sir, thank you kindly, Sir. It was good by your fire. It was as good a fire as I've seen this many a year.

SIR MARTIN

You see, gentlemen, that she is of a great simplicity. Alison Taylor, whether you have done anything or not, it is much easier to prove guilt even when it does not exist, than to prove innocence. But I will see that you have a fair trial and all the protection that the law allows. Gentlemen, the prisoner has been searched by the Witch Searcher in the presence of the Parson, the Physician and his wife, and the Witch Pricker, and no Devil's marks were found on her.

JUSTICE FEVER

Was she searched thoroughly in every part?

Physician

Yes, your Worship, and to my mind with grievous roughness.

Justice Fever

If they had been thorough they would have found something, that I know.

Upjohn

My case against the accused is that she, being a person from a distance, without occupation or address, and having no good business in this place, was making her way towards Sir Martin's house at the time (which she could have known) when he was due to return. Some of the sons of his tenants were trying to drive her off—you may think out of loyalty—when she was seen to shake her fist at the house, and thereafter to flatten herself in the ditch and from that position to make an unusually offensive sign which his Worship's horse could not pass. When urged, it threw him. Any injury to him would be a grievous blow to you all, loved as he is for his integrity and generosity. (*Murmurs of approval in the Court.*) You must all be shocked that anyone could wish him ill.

Sir Martin

It is yet to be proved that anyone did wish me ill. You must prove a motive.

Upjohn

I submit that your Worship's manifest goodness would be reason enough for the Devil's hatred.

Sir Martin

Fiddlesticks.

Upjohn

(*bowing*)

Your Worship is modest. With characteristic kindness, Sir Martin had Alison Taylor brought into his house for a meal, which she repaid by casting the Evil Eye, or as it is commonly called "overlooking" a little dog, the pet of the household, which has since died. (*Hostile murmurs.*)

When arrested three hours later she was eight miles away—you may wonder how she got so far—(*voice* "On a broomstick.") asleep in a hay-loft. A black cat was with her, which on seeing my men leapt through the window. One must not rule out the possibility of a "familiar" nor fail to imagine what blacker deeds, what more dreadful powers, may lurk behind the simple facts of the accusation that I bring.

Sir Martin

The simple facts of your accusation have yet to be proved. The blacker deeds are so far entirely imaginary. You can leave them out.

Upjohn

Your Worship. I will call my first witnesses.

Clerk

Mistress Philippa and Mistress Bess. You must take the oath. Hold the Holy Bible in your left hand. Without your gloves, please. Put your first finger on the text where the Bible is open and say after me—I swear before Almighty God—

Philippa

I swear before Almighty God—

CLERK

To speak the truth—

PHILIPPA

To speak the truth—

CLERK

The whole truth—

PHILIPPA

The whole truth—

CLERK

And nothing but the truth—

PHILIPPA

And nothing but the truth—

CLERK

So help me God.

PHILIPPA

So help me God.

CLERK

Mistress Bess. (*Repeats the oath with Bess.*)

SIR MARTIN
(*stands*)

My daughters, remember your immortal souls. (*Sits.*)

UPJOHN

Mistress Philippa, you are the eldest daughter of Sir Martin?

PHILIPPA

Yes.

UPJOHN

And you the second?

BESS

Yes.

UPJOHN

You have been brought up in this house?

PHILIPPA AND BESS

Yes.

UPJOHN

You revere him both as your father and as the good man we all know him to be?

PHILIPPA
(*startled and frightened*)

Yes.

BESS

Yes.

UPJOHN

Then your witness can hardly be doubted, coming from the honourable daughters of an honourable man. When did you first see the accused?

PHILIPPA

Through the window. The boys were trying to drive her away.

UPJOHN

She was quite near the house and you could see her clearly?

PHILIPPA AND BESS

Yes.

UPJOHN

What first aroused your suspicions?

PHILIPPA

She shook her fist at the house.

BESS

(*cautiously*)

I didn't see that.

UPJOHN

Did you see her go into the ditch?

PHILIPPA AND BESS

Yes. Yes.

UPJOHN

Did she fall?

PHILIPPA

She didn't exactly fall. She crouched like an animal and ran; and then she rolled over.

BESS

Yes, like that.

UPJOHN

On to her back?

PHILIPPA

Yes.

UPJOHN

Where she made this blasphemous sign?

BESS
(*inaudibly*)

Yes.

CLERK

Speak up, please.

PHILIPPA
(*looking full at Upjohn*)

Yes.

UPJOHN

Mistress Bess, you were very properly shocked. Did you see your father fall?

BESS

No. We had left the window.

UPJOHN

But you both saw him come in muddy and heard his explanation.

PHILIPPA AND BESS

Yes.

UPJOHN

I also have a statement from him. What happened when Alison Taylor came into the house?

PHILIPPA

Fido barked.

UPJOHN

It is said that dogs are particularly sensitive to the supernatural. The smell of her familiar may have been about her.

SIR MARTIN

The Court should remember that all dogs bark at all strangers. Which is why we keep them.

UPJOHN

But Alison Taylor showed an unusual dislike and fear of the dog?

PHILIPPA

She pointed at it . . .

BESS

And her face went all withered and screwed up like a monkey's, and she glared.

UPJOHN

What happened to the dog?

BESS

. . . it died (*almost inaudible*).

UPJOHN

It died.

(*Cries of* "Boo! Duck her! Hang her!")

It died. It might have been either of you. If this woman is a witch, and if she should be wrongfully acquitted, every witness at this trial, their Worships, myself, and every one of you in the crowd who has cried out against her, would be in danger. Remember that witches are seldom acting singly. Farmers say, "Where you see one rat there are a hundred unseen". I say, where you see one witch there are twelve more. They are a close society, or coven, able and keen to revenge each other. If this woman is a witch—I stress the if, as his Worship bids me—then there must be twelve more unsuspected witches among you now, working their dark and horrible deeds all the more freely because you have been too easy-going, too trustful. Think then for a moment. The hare that crosses your path in the fields; the chuckle of a jackdaw on your roof; the croak of a bull-frog behind you; the silent flight of owl or bat; the fearful yell of cats in the night; the laughter under the eaves; even the rustle of mice behind the wainscot may be the outward sign of that inward, invisible, spreading terror.

Justice Fever

Merciful heaven!

Francis

(stands with hand raised to command silence. Pause.)

I have kept this moment's silence because it seemed ungenerous to end Mr. Prosecutor's satisfaction in his own rolling rhetoric so soon with the little pin of common sense. When were Englishmen afraid of frogs and mice? Admittedly a dog has been poisoned. There is no evidence to show who did it, or if it was from something the dog picked up. I shall not cross-examine my two sisters at this point, because I know too well their talent for make-believe.

UPJOHN

My learned and juvenile friend is newly come from Cambridge, always a centre of that disbelief in spiritual powers, which he calls common sense. These are the opinions of youth. I am not much older myself, but I have already outgrown them. I will call the boys, none of whom have been corrupted with modern learning.

CLERK

Robert Ball, George Carp, Mat Price, Ben Goose, Tommy Vines. (*They take the oath all together like a school repetition.*)

SIR MARTIN

Do you understand what you have sworn?

BOYS

Yes, your Worship.

SIR MARTIN

Do you believe in God?

BOYS

Yes, your Worship.

SIR MARTIN

Then mind what you say.

UPJOHN

Now, boys, your parents are all tenants of Sir Martin?

BOYS

Yes, sir.

Upjohn

You all know him and respect him?

Boys

Yes, sir.

Upjohn

You would not willingly let anyone harm him?

Boys

No, sir.

Upjohn

You did in fact try to drive Alison Taylor away from his gate? (*Surprise.*)

Robert

Yes, sir. (*The others all look at him.*)

Upjohn

You were the leader in coming to his Worship's defence?

Robert

Yes, sir.

Sir Martin

Mr. Prosecutor, I cannot allow it to be thought that pelting an old woman with mud and stones can ever earn my gratitude. Boys will pelt anything. It could as easily have been my windows, and often is.

Upjohn

Your Worship. Where did you first see the wi— . . . this woman?

ROBERT

About half a mile back.

UPJOHN

What made you suspect her?

GEORGE

She was a foreigner.

MAT

Foreigners is up to no good.

GEORGE

We don't want them.

UPJOHN

What was she doing?

MAT

Talking to herself.

BEN GOOSE

An' talking to a cat on the wall.

UPJOHN

Was she, indeed? Did she *fondle* it particularly? Could you hear what she said to it?

BEN

A' scratched it under the chin and mumbled a lot of silly stuff.

UPJOHN

It might not have seemed so silly if you had understood it. Did the cat seem to know her?

BEN

It arched its back and held its tail up like they do. (*Draws it in the air tail last, as if stroking it.*)

UPJOHN

Did it seem to be hers?

TOMMY

Please, sir, it was my auntie's cat. (*Laughter.*)

UPJOHN

Be careful, little boy, how you bring your auntie into this. Two witches often share a familiar devil, which may be in the form of a cat.

TOMMY

My auntie's not a witch, and she hasn't got a devil. (*Laughter.*)

UPJOHN

This little witness is not yet very wise about women. Not many married men would agree with him. (*Laughter.*) Have you ever seen the Devil, Tommy?

TOMMY

No, sir.

UPJOHN

Then how would you recognise him if you saw him? Now, boys. Was the old woman making straight for Sir Martin's house?

ROBERT

Yes, sir.

UPJOHN

And you couldn't get her to change her direction?

ROBERT

No, sir.

UPJOHN

Did she hiss or spit at you?

BEN

She mewed like a cat when a mud ball hit her in the mouth. (*Boys titter.*)

UPJOHN

Come now, this is a serious matter. When she was by the house, did she show any hostility?

ROBERT, GEORGE, MAT AND BEN

(*in chorus as if taught*)

She shook her fist at it.

TOMMY

But that was because . . .

UPJOHN

That's enough, Tommy. My question has been answered.

SIR MARTIN

Mr. Prosecutor, I think we should hear what this very spontaneous witness has to say. Go on, Tommy. That was because?

TOMMY

Because the young lady was throwing at her too, out of the window.

(*Boys nudge him and whisper* "Justice's daughter, you daft little . . . ")

SIR MARTIN

Which young lady, Tommy? Don't be afraid.

(*Tommy points silently at Bess. Murmurs in the crowd.*)

SIR MARTIN

(*wearily*)

Question her, Mr. Prosecutor.

UPJOHN

I would like to submit that the last witness is too young to be of any reliability in Court.

Mistress Bess, what do you say to this unlikely suggestion from our little witness? For my part your grace and good breeding make it quite impossible to believe.

BESS

I was eating an apple and it had a maggot in it, so I opened the lattice and threw it out.

PHILIPPA

That's right. And the old woman had shaken her fist before the apple was thrown away.

UPJOHN

I think I have made my point.

FRANCIS

I shall not take much of the Court's time in dismissing my learned friend's fairy story about a heroic band of boys confronting the Devil. It was quite a feat to make so much out of so little. What? A lonely old woman stops to stroke a cat? Which of us can resist a cat that asks to be stroked, as Ben Goose so neatly showed us? You will hardly condemn anyone to death for that. As for the ominous shaken fist, would it not have been natural to shake it at any one of those plaguing boys? For that is all they were. Just idle young bullies.

VOICE

Don't you call our Robert a bully.

VOICE

What about your sister?

UPJOHN

Call my next witness.

CLERK

Mistress Jenny.

(Jenny takes the oath quietly and without prompting.)

UPJOHN

Did you see the prisoner, Alison Taylor, in your father's ante-room?

JENNY

Yes, sir.

UPJOHN

Did your dog Fido bark at her?

JENNY

Yes, sir, just a woof.

UPJOHN

He was not a very good watch dog?

JENNY

Yes, sir, he was.

UPJOHN

Why, if it was only one woof! as you say, was she so vexed?

JENNY

There were dogs with the boys outside, and they had been fierce. I heard them.

UPJOHN

So she was vexed?

JENNY

I think she was frightened.

UPJOHN

Did she then point her finger at Fido?

JENNY

Yes. And I picked him up.

UPJOHN

Nevertheless, she cast the Evil Eye on him?

JENNY

She didn't look any different from anyone else.

UPJOHN

But all the same Fido died?

(*Jenny weeps.*)

He died, didn't he?

(*She nods.*)

(*Rhythmic sounds of* "Witch, Witch, Witch, Witch".)

UPJOHN

Thank you. I need not ask you any more.

FRANCIS

Jenny, you are very sad about Fido; but do you really believe it was the Evil Eye that killed him?

JENNY

No. My sisters are always making up stories. I can't believe the real Devil was peeping out from under the old woman's skirts.

(*Murmurs of excitement and belief, in which Fever joins.*)

Or that he jumped up the chimney. Nobody over three could believe that.

FRANCIS

Is that what your sisters said?

JENNY

Yes. Bess said she jerked the old woman's stool away to make the Devil run out, and Philippa said she saw him leap up the chimney. Who would believe that?

FRANCIS

Some grown-up people would.

JENNY

They must be very silly people.

FRANCIS

So you don't believe any of it?

JENNY

No.

FRANCIS

Thank you, Jenny. That's all.

UPJOHN

Mistress Philippa. Your sister Jenny has cast doubts upon the evidence that you gave under oath. I think you should be given the chance of clearing away any suspicion of perjury that might arise. Though your sister Jenny is very young to give evidence in Court, yet suspicion sticks. I should be sorry to see so beautiful and promising a young lady as yourself dishonoured, and her whole future blighted for want of instant confirmation of the evidence. Let us look for it.

Do you agree that Mistress Bess, suspecting the Devil, pulled away the stool from under the prisoner?

PHILIPPA

Yes, sir, she did.

UPJOHN

And did the prisoner fall?

PHILIPPA

Yes, she did. And spilt all her soup.

UPJOHN

Did she not hurt herself?

PHILIPPA

She hurt her elbow.

UPJOHN

But you yourself did the prisoner no personal injury?

PHILIPPA

No.

UPJOHN

Is it not odd that after such an affront from your sister Bess, the prisoner should have cast the Evil Eye on Fido, who is dead, and not rather on your sister? Was she not the obvious victim?

PHILIPPA

Oh. She cast it on Bess too.
(*Dead silence in the Court.*)

BESS

You couldn't! You wouldn't dare!

UPJOHN

She cast it on Bess too.
(*Bess falls in a dead faint.*)
We cannot doubt that she did.
(*Uproar in the Court. Cries of "Duck the Witch, Duck the Witch, Duck the Witch". The Physician comes to Bess and he and Alice carry her out, followed by Jenny.*)

Girth, Fever and De Groot
(*after conferring, to Sir Martin*)

Let the prisoner be taken and ducked.

Justice de Groot

Let her be ducked first and hanged afterwards.

Sir Martin

I cannot agree with you, gentlemen. That the guilty float and the innocent sink, is a theory impossible of proof. But you overrule me. Constables, let Alison Taylor be taken and ducked, but see that she has fair treatment. Afterwards let her be taken back to her cell. The trial is adjourned till tomorrow. Go with them, Parson, and use your influence. Francis, go and do what you can. See that the rope is good, and if they don't drown her, give her this cordial. Mr. Mayor?

(*The Mayor shrugs. Constables lead out Alison Taylor. The Justices go out, the Court clears in wild excitement. Mr. Upjohn offers his arm to Philippa.*)

Upjohn

Shall we go and watch?

A Furtive Man

Sir, you'll find a name writ here that might interest you, but I'd be glad if mine need not come into it.

Upjohn

I'll look into it. (*Tips him.*)
Come, my young beauty. Let's see the sport.

Curtain

Scene II

The ante-room.

Bess lying on a bench in front of the fire. Alice, Jenny and Physician slapping Bess's hand.

Physician

It is a very deep faint.

Alice

It is just the excitement of the Court. At her age it is quite usual. (*Slaps her face.*)
Bess! Bess!!

Physician

Her pulse is low. Burnt feathers might bring her round.

Alice

Run, Jenny, to the kitchen. There are pheasants there.
(*Exit Jenny.*)

Physician

It was a very strange attack, happening like that. It has doomed that old creature.
(*Re-enter Jenny with feathers.*)
Her pulse flutters. There, that's better. She's coming round.
Dame Alice, some hot milk and brandy, if you can.

Bess

Oh, Jenny! Stay with me, Jenny. Don't let them do it. I know they mean to.

Jenny

Do what, Bess? You are still dreaming.

BESS

I'm frightened. Stay, Jenny. Never leave me alone.

(*Re-enter Alice.*)

ALICE

Drink this, Bess. You'll feel better.

BESS

What is it? Milk! No, no. I won't.

ALICE

Come along. The Physician says you are to have it. (*Tries to make her drink.*)

BESS

No no no no. (*Fights.*)

PHYSICIAN

We won't force her, lest she faint again. Let her rest, and her sister stay by her.

(*Bess weeps with her face in the pillow.*)

She'll do now.

(*Wild shouts outside.*)

I may be wanted after the ducking. Shall we go? You wouldn't want to miss it.

ALICE

No, indeed.

(*Exeunt Physician and Alice, right.*)

JENNY

What is it, Bess?

BESS

I'm so frightened. Oh, Jenny, I'm sorry about Fido. I really am. I don't want to see Philippa.

JENNY

She's gone to the ducking.

(*Second round of shouting, then dead silence. Jenny rises as if to go to the window.*)

BESS

(*clutching*)

Stay with me, Jenny. I'm frightened of Philippa. And Alice. And Mr. Upjohn. They are all bad. I want Father. I'm not frightened of him. I know he's terribly angry with me, but he would never do anything bad. I know he wouldn't.

(*Wild shouting, continuous and approaching.*)

BESS

Don't go.

(*Enter Sir Martin, sternly.*)

SIR MARTIN

Well, Bess. Was this play-acting?

BESS

(*into pillow*)

No, Father.

JENNY

It was a bad faint, Father. She was so long coming round, I couldn't help wondering if she was . . . like Fido.

(*Bess sobs.*)

SIR MARTIN

You have done a bad day's work, and if this faint was feigned, it was the Devil's own idea.

BESS

It wasn't pretence, really it wasn't. It had got too horrible. Father! I need you. I don't mind what you do to me.

SIR MARTIN

If this is repentance, it is good, though it comes too late. Real or pretence, your faint has doomed poor old Alison.

JENNY

There was such a dreadful shouting, Father. What has happened?

SIR MARTIN

I was glad you were not there, my love, to see such barbarity. They stripped her and tied her hands and feet and threw her in, and she sank. Then she came up again three times, as they say all drowning persons do, and Francis pulled her out. Then Fever and De Groot said "Throw her in again". They did, poor old thing. She was blue and shivering—it was bitterly cold. This time she only came up twice but was pulled out coughing.

JENNY

And then?

SIR MARTIN

And then that scoundrel Upjohn inflamed the crowd so that they clamoured for a third trial. And Francis said, in that case he would be thrown in too, in the same way, so that they could compare his sinking with hers. The two

Constables tied him and threw him in, and Walter and the Kennelman held the ropes. You must have heard the shouting then. The old woman had no breath left in her old body at all, and she sank like a stone, but Francis's back floated like a raft though his face was under water. However, the Kennelman looked after him, and he's all right.

JENNY

And old Alison?

SIR MARTIN

Walter pulled her out. The Parson and the Physician did what they could do to get the water out of her, and Francis shared his brandy with her. That dreadful Witch Searcher dressed her and they took her away to her cell. There'll be no fire there to warm her.

JENNY

Couldn't we send her one?

SIR MARTIN

My darling child! Yes, we could.
Walter! Walter!
(*Enter Walter.*)

WALTER

Yes, Sir?

SIR MARTIN

Tell the blacksmith to get the brazier out of the armoury and take it down to the lock-up, with a good barrow of small logs, to make a fire for the prisoner. Here's a shilling for the Turnkey. Tell him I sent you. And do you get a basket of food from Cook and take that to her. She is not yet proved guilty.

WALTER

I'll be glad to do it, Sir. The old woman was more dead than alive. She takes it all as patient and helpless as an ill-used dog. I don't like to see it.

SIR MARTIN

You're a good boy, Walter. You did all you could for her.

(*Exit Walter. Enter Philippa pink-cheeked and laughing, followed by Alice.*)

PHILIPPA

What an afternoon! I haven't laughed so much for ages. Pity you weren't there, Bess. I couldn't have laughed more, unless they'd thrown in Father and the Bishop instead of Francis.

(*Sees her father and scoots upstairs. Exit via gallery left.*)

SIR MARTIN

Wretched girl. Does innocence and injustice mean nothing to you? Mistress Alice, have you no influence on her?

ALICE

I do my best, Sir, but girls of that age will not be told anything. How should she listen to me if she will not listen to you?

SIR MARTIN

Because you are young, and a woman.

(*Enter Francis.*)

Well done, my son. Come to the fire. I am sure you need it.

FRANCIS

I am warmer now, thank you, Sir. The water felt as cold as a sword. (*To Bess*) Well, sister, your ill-timed faint turned everyone against us. Why did you have to faint just at that moment? I have to thank you for my ducking. Forgive me for getting between you and the fire. You'd better be cured by Monday.

ALICE

I will see that she has plenty of good food and cordials. I shall make it my business.

BESS

No. No. I don't want anything. I won't eat anything.

SIR MARTIN

You will do as you are told.

BESS

I can't, Father.

SIR MARTIN

She should be in bed in her room. Take her up, Mistress Alice.

BESS

Not with Philippa. Please, please, Father, not with Philippa. Please, Father, let me be in Jenny's room.

ALICE

Girls! Girls! One whim after another. Come with me, Bess.

Sir Martin

I should not wish to be with Philippa myself, after her exhibition today. Jenny, will you have Bess with you?

Jenny

Yes, I'll look after her.

Bess

Thank you, Jenny.
(*Enter Upjohn.*)
Don't leave me.

Upjohn

Well, Master Francis. I have never had that trick played on me by Defence before. You are full of ingenuity. It was a blow to our three Justices. They will talk of nothing else till Monday, and probably for a year after. There's nothing like making a real show of it. The whole neighbourhood will be buzzing. They don't often have the chance to see the Squire's son sail through the air and go in splosh. Incidentally, you wet me through. This story will get to London and make laughing stocks of us both. And how is our little invalid? You have won our case for us.

(*Bess starts away but fails to get on her feet.*)

Jenny

Help me please, Francis. We'll take her up to my room.
(*Francis carries her up. Exeunt.*)

Sir Martin

Excuse me, Mr. Upjohn, if I go to my room till supper. I am very tired and I think we have little to say to each other. You have a good fire. Tobacco here if you have a pipe. Mistress Alice will bring you wine.

(*Exit, centre back.*)

Upjohn

We will drink to our success so far, Alice. I have been given three more names today. Here. Look at these. Are any of them our people?

Alice

These? No! Contemptible envy and childish revenges. Nothings.

Upjohn

Seeds then of large harvests. Look at our good Justice Martin and his daughters. May his heart break! (*Pours a second glass.*) To old Chaos.

Alice
(*drinks to him*)

My Lord!

Upjohn

It will be Candlemas on Monday. Where do you meet?

Alice

On Herne Fen.

UPJOHN

The Grand Master will be attending. (*Deep reverence from Alice.*)

At what time can you leave?

ALICE

A little before midnight. But I must be back by cock-crow.

UPJOHN

You ride behind me on the Black Horse. On Herne Fen we will dance together the Dance of the Horned Beasts.

CURTAIN

Scene III

The Court Room. Two days later.

The second day of the trial is in progress. The Justices are sitting. Witnesses, notables, crowds, constables as before. Alison Taylor mumbles continuously as if in delirium. Alice, Cook and the Kennelman are the only witnesses. Philippa with notables.

Sir Martin

Let the prisoner be seated. It is clear she can hardly stand. (*Constable brings her a stool.*)

Old Mother

Let me sit by the fire. There's nothing like a good fire.

Upjohn

Your Worships, it must be admitted, however reluctantly, that the ordeal by water gave no clear proof of the prisoner's guilt. And though Sir Martin's Kennelman was of the opinion that the dog died by poison, it must be remembered that witches are skilled in poison and can kill at a distance by sending a familiar flea to inject it into the victim's veins.

(*Fever huddles up into his cloak and signs to the Court to stand back from the prisoner.*)

The witness of Sir Martin's Cook confirms that Mistress Bess both insulted and injured the prisoner. We must therefore give great weight to Mistress Alice's account of that young lady.

Mistress Alice, how is his Worship's daughter Bess since her seizure in the Court here on Saturday?

Alice

She is very ill. She has had no food or drink these three days. She cannot swallow and spits out all we give her.

Upjohn

What reason does she give for refusing food and drink?

Alice

She will not speak nor answer, either to me or to her eldest sister Philippa, though till now they were never apart.

Upjohn

Is her mind affected?

Alice

She has fits of unreason and screams if approached.

Upjohn

How does she receive her father?

Alice

She covers her face with the bedclothes.

Upjohn

Your Worships, this is surely as clear a case of the Evil Eye as you are ever likely to hear of. It is as if the Devil, resenting her father's manifest disbelief, should strike down a daughter of the house to prove his power.

Francis

It is at least as likely that my sister Bess, who is only twelve years old, should be violently repenting her silly stories on seeing where they lead. Look, your Worships, and all of you in the court room at that poor old woman there.

(*Alison Taylor has stopped muttering and wheezing and sits huddled and bent, her head nearly on her knees.*)

She should rather have been given a pension and found a room in an almshouse than be treated with the in-humanity we have all seen. I implore you, find more mercy in your hearts than fear.

Sir Martin

Gentlemen, we have heard all the evidence and must now agree on our decision. I am bitterly ashamed of my two daughters, and for my part do not believe a word that they have said.

Justice Fever

But the dog was bewitched, and your daughter, too. You can't overlook that. Do you not care for your own daughter? Then how can you care for the rest of us? My blood runs cold.

Justice Girth

She has done two bewitchments, that's a fact. They can't both be coincidence.

Justice de Groot

There's no two ways about it. She is guilty, without any doubt, of the worst crime there is. She should suffer the worst punishment. She should be hanged.

Sir Martin

It is not in the power of this Court to pass sentence. You are three to one. Do you wish her to be kept in prison until the Assizes and re-tried then?

Girth, Fever and De Groot

We do.

Sir Martin

I wish to dissociate myself from my three colleagues who find the evidence against the prisoner sufficient.

Alison Taylor, you have been presumed guilty of witch-craft and are to be confined in prison until the Assizes.

(*Uproar in Court and a minute later cheering outside.*)

Constable, take the prisoner back to her cell.

(*The Constable shakes Alison Taylor by the shoulder and she falls to the floor.*)

Constable

Your Worships—she's dead.

Justice de Groot

Why, damnation, she can't be hanged if she's dead!

(*Physician comes forward—confusion. Outside the cheering has changed to a sound like the buzzing of bees.*)

Curtain

Scene IV

The ante-room.

Walter in attendance. Enter right Sir Martin, Francis, Parson, Physician.

Sir Martin

It is good of you, my old friends, to come in with me tonight. I need your company. Why could they not have shown her some sympathy before she died? You would think now that she was everybody's grandmother.

Francis

These are people I have grown up among, and they enjoyed the ducking like a day's sport. I shall never feel the same to them again.

(*Enter Jenny from upstairs with a mug. Curtsies to all as she goes.*)

Sir Martin

Here is one who will always be the same. Where are you off to, my love?

Jenny

I am getting some milk for Bess. She will take what I give her, if I get it myself.

(*Exit to kitchen and then upstairs.*)

Francis

I suspect Philippa and Bess of more guilt than we know.

Sir Martin

Don't speak to me of them. I fear I must find another housekeeper. For all her breeding, she fails to have the right influence. Come, my friends—in here.

(*Exeunt centre back.*)

(*Enter right Alice and Philippa. Upjohn's back can be partly seen in entrance right. Alice goes through into the kitchen left. Philippa hangs about waiting for Upjohn. He enters but does not ac-knowledge her bob curtsy. She runs forward.*)

Philippa

Wasn't it splendid? You won your case. I knew you would, of course. And I did help, didn't I?

Upjohn

Did I ask you your help?

Philippa

No, of course you didn't. But I gave it, didn't I! You could say thank you.

Upjohn

(*bowing*)

Too kind.

Philippa

Isn't that what you wanted? Aren't you pleased?

UPJOHN

Pleased! You brainless girl, can't you see that now she's dead all the sympathy is turned the other way? Nobody will be found now to incriminate their neighbours—until they've forgotten the old hag. It's her ghost they'll fear now. And so should you. If only she had lived long enough to be hanged.

PHILIPPA

But it wasn't my fault that she died. You are unfair.

UPJOHN

Unfair! Unfair! Do you think I bother about being fair, you nonentity? Were you fair to the old creature? Hang them all! I want spectacular results.

PHILIPPA

Oh.

UPJOHN

I'll be as unfair as the law allows, but it will be a waste of time here for—weeks. I don't waste weeks. I shall be moving on tonight.

PHILIPPA

Tonight? You're not going? For always?

UPJOHN

With your permission.

PHILIPPA

Take me with you. You can't leave me with Father. I don't know what he will do to me. Let me come with you. Take me. It was all only for you.

UPJOHN

You are tiresome. Tell your father, with my most reverent compliments of course, that I am dining with Justice de Groot this evening before leaving. My servants will come for my baggage. Adieu, Mistress Philippa.

(*Exit right. Philippa runs upstairs and throws herself weeping on her bed.*)

CURTAIN

Scene V

The ante-room, later that night.

Moonlight through window right. The house in darkness. Enter above, Alice carrying a candle. She is wearing a mask and a hood. She comes down slowly, sets the door right ajar, puts out the candle. Presently the door is pushed open and bright moonlight throws on a screen the shadow of Upjohn in a bull's mask. Enter Upjohn.

Upjohn

The fire is lit. It is time. Come, they are waiting for us.

Alice

I have a good account to give them. I have tonight done what must be done to raise a ghost. (*Laughs.*)

Upjohn

You are never idle. Is it to plague that idiot girl?

Alice

It was not difficult, being but a poor spirit and hardly yet detached. I charged it with the power and malice that it lacked. It will plague her.

Upjohn

Well done. You have a pleasant genius for evil.

Alice

The Horned Man is my god.

(*Exeunt.*)

Curtain

Scene VI

The girls' bedroom.

Sounds of horse galloping into distance. Silence. Upstairs alone in her room, Philippa, weeping, lights her candle.

PHILIPPA

I can't bear it. I'm so miserable. I wish Bess was here. God! I might have poisoned her if he had needed it. How could he be so cruel? What shall I do? Father will send me away. Nobody loves me. He doesn't. Oh, oh I can't believe it. I must talk to somebody. I shall go mad.

(*Gets up and knocks on door.*)

Alice! Alice! (*Opens door.*) Alice!

She's not there! I am all alone. Where can she be? The night seems to have stopped moving, it will never end. It's as if somebody had made a hole in time. Brr! I've got the shudders. Perhaps I can see the time on the church clock by moonlight.

(*From her bed pulls the curtain and opens the window.*)

There's a fire somewhere over there. The clouds are red underneath. There's something going on somewhere. I can feel it. But not here. It's the Nothingness that's going on here that frightens me. Aah! I'm young and I'm pretty and I'm alive, and he has left me. It's all because of that old dead hag. What did she matter anyway? She was old.

(*Twelve o'clock strikes.*)

What's that rustling in the ivy?

(*Pushing through the lattice comes the fumbling black bundle of the old woman's ghost. It crouches like an animal.*)

(*Philippa tries to scream but almost no sound comes.*)

CURTAIN

Acknowledgements

With many thanks to Diana Boston,
Meggan Kehrli, Robert Lloyd Parry, Albert Power,
Jim Rockhill, Ray Russell and Brian J. Showers.

Curfew & Other Eerie Tales was first
published by Swan River Press
in September 2010.

"Curfew" was first published in
The House of the Nightmare and Other Eerie Tales
Edited by Kathleen Lines
London: Bodley Head, 1967

"Many Coloured Glass" was first published in
Young Winter's Tales
Edited by M. R. Hodgkin
London: Macmillan, 1970

The Horned Man was first published by
London: Faber and Faber, 1970

"The Tiger-Skin Rug" was first published in
Dread and Delight: A Century of Children's Ghost Stories
Edited by Philippa Pearce
Oxford: Oxford University Press, 1995

"Pollution", "Blind Man's Buff" and "The Italian Desk"
appear here for the first time.

About the Author

Lucy M. Boston (1892–1990) was born in Southport, Lancashire. She studied English at Oxford and served as a nurse in France, before settling in Cheshire towards the end of the First World War. After her marriage broke down in 1935 she trained as a painter in Europe, eventually returning to England on the eve of the Second World War. In 1939 she bought the eleventh century Manor in Hemingford Grey, Cambridgeshire, which was her home and literary inspiration until her death. It is the setting of her much-loved series of Green Knowe novels for children, and is now open to visitors.

SWAN RIVER PRESS

Founded in 2003, Swan River Press is an independent publishing company, based in Dublin, Ireland, dedicated to gothic, supernatural, and fantastic literature. We special-ise in limited edition hardbacks, publishing fiction from around the world with an emphasis on Ireland's contribu-tions to the genre.

www.swanriverpress.ie

"Handsome, beautifully made volumes . . . altogether irresistible."

– Michael Dirda, *Washington Post*

"It [is] often down to small, independent, specialist presses to keep the candle of horror fiction flickering . . . "

– Darryl Jones, *Irish Times*

"Swan River Press has emerged as one of the most inspiring new presses over the past decade. Not only are the books beautifully presented and professionally produced, but they aspire consistently to high literary quality and originality, ranging from current writers of supernatural/weird fiction to rare or forgotten works by departed authors."

– Peter Bell, *Ghosts & Scholars*

GHOSTS OF THE CHIT-CHAT

edited by Robert Lloyd Parry

On the evening of Saturday, 28 October 1893, Cambridge University's Chit-Chat Club convened its 601st meeting. Ten members and one guest gathered in the rooms of Montague Rhodes James, the Junior Dean of King's College, and listened—with increasing absorption one suspects—as their host read "Two Ghost Stories".

Ghosts of the Chit-Chat celebrates this momentous event in the history of supernatural literature, the earliest dated record we have of M. R. James reading his ghost stories out loud. And it revives the contributions that other members made to the genre; men of imagination who invoked the ghostly in their work, and who are now themselves shades. In a series of essays, stories, and poems Robert Lloyd Parry looks at the history and culture of the Club.

In addition to tales and poems never before reprinted, *Ghosts of the Chit-Chat* features earlier, slightly different versions of two of M. R. James's best-known ghost stories; Robert Lloyd Parry's profiles and commentaries on each featured Chit-Chat member sheds new light on this supernatural tradition, making *Ghosts of the Chit-Chat* a valuable resource for casual readers and long-time Jamesians alike.

"An exquisite reading pleasure."

– Black Gate

"This is a lovely little book . . . there are some fascinating and often rarely seen pieces of writing here."

– A Ghostly Company

EARTH-BOUND
and Other Supernatural Tales

Dorothy Macardle

Originally published in 1924, the nine tales that comprise Earth-Bound were written by Dorothy Macardle while she was held a political prisoner in Dublin's Kilmainham Gaol and Mountjoy Prison. The stories incorporate themes that intrigued her throughout her life; themes out of the myths and legends of Ireland; ghostly interventions, dreams and premonitions, clairvoyance, and the Otherworld in parallel with this one. It is so easy to dismiss them, as some have, merely as part of the narrative of "Irish nationalism" of the time, but it is the supernatural elements that make them much more. She would revisit these themes in later works such as her classic haunted house novel *The Uninvited* (1941). To this new edition of Macardle's debut collection, reprinted for the first time in ninety years, we have added four more tales of the supernatural.

"Beautifully written, with a fine air for the music of language and vivid descriptions of the landscape."

– Black Static

"A beautifully presented and valuable resource for anyone interested in Irish history, culture or literature."

– Dublin Inquirer

BENDING TO EARTH
Strange Stories by Irish Women

edited by Maria Giakaniki
and Brian J. Showers

Irish women have long produced literature of the gothic, uncanny, and supernatural. *Bending to Earth* draws together twelve such tales. While none of the authors herein were considered primarily writers of fantastical fiction during their lifetimes, they each wandered at some point in their careers into more speculative realms—some only briefly, others for lengthier stays.

Names such as Charlotte Riddell and Rosa Mulholland will already be familiar to aficionados of the eerie, while Katharine Tynan and Clotilde Graves are sure to gain new admirers. From a ghost story in the Swiss Alps to a premonition of death in the West of Ireland to strange rites in a South Pacific jungle, *Bending to Earth* showcases a diverse range of imaginative writing which spans the better part of a century.

> "Bending to Earth *is full of tales of women walled-up in rooms, of vengeful or unforgetting dead wives, of mistreated lovers, of cruel and murderous husbands.*"
>
> – Darryl Jones, *Irish Times*

> "*A surprising, extraordinary anthology featuring twelve uncanny and supernatural stories from the nineteenth century . . . highly recommended, extremely enjoyable.*"
>
> – British Fantasy Society